Mystic TIDES

C.J. GODWIN

outskirtspress

DENVER, COLORADO

Mystic Tides
All Rights Reserved.
Copyright © 2016 C.J. Godwin
v3.0

Cover Photo © 2016 thinkstockphotos.com. All rights reserved - used with permission.

Outskirts Press, Inc.
http://www.outskirtspress.com

ISBN: 978-1-4787-0137-8

Outskirts Press and the "OP" logo are trademarks belonging to Outskirts Press, Inc.

PRINTED IN THE UNITED STATES OF AMERICA

Acknowledgements

Special thanks to my coach and editor
Rob Carr
as well as to my amazing sister
Courtney Love
for all of her help.

I also want to thank my wonderful husband
Bryan
as well as my mother, father, brother, Ariel Jacobs
and all of my family and friends
for their love and support.

I hope you all enjoy reading my story
as much as I enjoyed writing it.

Contents

Prologue

"I found him!" Nitra exclaimed to her mother, beaming with pride.

"Are you sure that it's him?" Vanessa asked, gripping her daughter's arm so tightly that she could feel her pulse. She was barely able to contain her excitement. "How do you know for sure?"

Nitra nodded her head up and down. "I don't exactly know how to explain it. The closer you get to him, the more you can just feel it. The power that radiates off of him, it's magnetic, like the gravitational force of the moon."

Vanessa pondered this for a moment. Although she had not witnessed this force herself, it did seem like it would be correct, a power that he would possess if he were indeed the one, based on the information that Maggie had passed along to her. She could hardly believe it! They had been searching for him for almost a year. Now they finally had him.

She couldn't believe her luck. First her brother shows up, bringing her the most amazing and unexpected gifts, now this! She could feel the wheels beginning to turn in her head as the final pieces to her master plan began to fall into place. Her smile widened wickedly as she imagined the end result.

Vanessa looked pointedly at her daughter. "So, I just have one more question for you."

Nitra looked at her mother, briefly wondering to herself if it were possible that he could be dangerous. Her mother's eyes widened with expectancy as she relayed her daughters instructions.

"What are you waiting for? Go get him!!!"

Chapter 1

Moonstone

I 've always wondered why most people are so drawn to the ocean. Some believe that we were once a part of it, that the majority of us evolved over time to become more acclimated to the land. That is why it speaks to us, calls to us, at a deep, primal level. Our instincts may still feel what our minds no longer remember, or perhaps there's another reason...

I sat on the black, rocky shores of Kenai beach, watching the full moon reflect off the waves of Cook Inlet. I could see the white, snow-capped peaks of the Chignit Mountains, up over the waters, in the distance. Their jagged edges rose majestically in the scenic backdrop, seeming to glow mysteriously in the bright, incandescent moonlight.

The night itself was so clear that I could see every vivid star in the sky twinkling peacefully in the heavens above me. The stars themselves reminded me of tiny diamonds the way that they sparkled, contrasting starkly against the black velvet of the nocturnal sky.

I had grown up slowly in this place, an environment that was more nature than town. Even though I'd lived here my entire life, it never ceased to amaze me how small and insignificant one could feel while sitting beside the ocean.

Today had been a special day. It was my seventeenth birthday. Earlier, all of my friends whom I'd known since childhood had thrown me a huge bonfire bash here on the beach. As much fun as we'd had drinking hot chocolate and dancing to nostalgic tunes, it had been bittersweet for this was also my going away party. Tonight was my last night in Alaska.

Now, alone on the beach, my thoughts turned to my best friend Abby. Cute, sweet, funny Abigail. We had been inseparable since that day in kindergarten when I stood up for her on the playground as Ben kept pulling her pigtails. I had often wondered to myself if there could ever possibly be something more to our friendship, for she had been the closest thing that I'd ever had to having a girlfriend, but I would never allow it. I was too afraid to lose her if things didn't work out.

I would always keep my distance whenever it felt like we were getting too close. Like tonight, she had offered to stay with me earlier as the party began to wane, but I told her that I would be okay. She should go home because it was getting late. I said that I just wanted to spend some time by myself.

We had then said our goodbyes, promised to keep in touch and hugged each other for what seemed like forever. I tried my best not to think about how much I was going to miss her. I remembered looking down at her as she was staring up at me with tears in her eyes. It almost seemed as if she'd wanted me to kiss her. But I couldn't be sure and was too hesitant. The moment had come, then just as quickly it had passed. Now I would always have to wonder what might have been.

As the fire began to die, I watched the tide coming in and my mind began to drift to my father, Brogan. He had been born and raised in Kenai and taught me everything I knew about hunting and fishing, but also to respect nature and the animals.

"Only kill it if you're going to eat it" he had advised me at a young age, along with "If you must take a life, do it as quickly and humanely as possible."

I had been a natural with the bow and arrow and after only a little bit of training my skills had quickly surpassed his. I'll never forget the expression on his face the day he saw me hit a target the size of a quarter at a distance of five hundred yards. It was priceless. As I became able to attain complete concentration, I never missed.

When his confidence in me began to grow he began to place bets with some of his buddies. After a while, as the word spread around the town, no one was foolish enough to agree to give up their hard-earned cash.

Like my father, I was tall and slim, yet muscular with a light tan. We both had dark black hair, but I kept mine slightly longer with the straight tips of it gently brushing my thick lashes that outlined my silvery grey eyes.

"You have your mother's eyes," I remember my father had once said.

My mother had left me on his doorstep when I was just a baby. He told me that it had been a complete shock to him, for he never knew that she was pregnant. She had left him suddenly nine months before.

Though I would often sit and try to recall something about her, I didn't remember her at all. The only thing I knew was that her name was Melissa. No last name, just Melissa. Whenever I asked questions about her, my dad would talk about how beautiful and strong and smart she was. Then he would become depressed for several days after.

He said that he had fallen head over heels with her instantly and had become so infatuated that he never even bothered to ask all of the important questions that normal people ask when they are getting to know someone, like, "Where are you from?, How old are you?, What's your freaking last name?!!"

Despite the strange circumstances, I thought my dad was doing a pretty good job raising me as a single parent, with the occasional help from my nearby grandparents.

However, my whole life changed a few months ago when my father had gotten a big promotion. He told me that toward the end of the summer, I would be going to live down in Florida with my erratic Aunt Tess and her only daughter Alana.

At first I had been furious.

"It's my senior year!"

That had basically been my only argument.

We fought for weeks, back and forth to no avail. Finally I just gave in, resigning myself to the inevitable outcome.

As a local fisherman my father had always been able to provide a meager, yet sufficient income for us. At the same time he had always dreamed of working on one of those offshore crab boats where, despite the danger, the money was significantly better.

"Then I could afford to send you to any college that you wished to attend," he'd told me, trying to win my approval.

For years he had been stuck on a waiting list and now that his opportunity had finally arrived, I no longer had the heart to try and talk him out of it.

Continuing to gaze out at the ocean, releasing a sigh, I returned to the moment and thought about the thing that I would miss the most about Alaska. Besides my friends and my father, it would have to be the sense of adventure, being in the wilderness where anything could happen at any given moment. A place where the air was so fresh and pure that I could breathe deeply without the worry of any of the modern day toxins.

The thing that I would miss the least were the bleak, frigid winters. Most people hated the extremely long nights that came along with that desolate time of year, a time when the sun would only come out for four hours at a time, but not me, I loved it! Under the cover of night I felt the most alive, the most at peace. I just wished that it wasn't so dang cold!

As I continued to watch the ever turning waves, I thought about how dramatically my life was about to change.

If only I had known then just how true that thought really was.

I felt a cool, strange breeze blow in from across the water. It gave me goose bumps, making the hair on the back of my neck suddenly stand on end. Instinctively I knew that something wasn't quite right. I could somehow feel that I was in immediate danger and at that very moment of realization, the remnants of my fire abruptly went dark.

I could hear a lone wolf howling in the distance and I looked toward the woods on the top of the hill to my right. I could tell from the faintness of the noise that the animal was too far away to be the threat that I had felt. It had to be something else.

As my eyes adjusted to the darkness that surrounded me, I glanced back to the ocean and saw a strange flash of red and orange dance atop a moonlit wave. Then just as quickly it disappeared.

In all of the years that I'd spent outdoors, near the sea, I had never seen a fish, whale or any other animal that looked even remotely like that. My curiosity was piqued, but there was also a fear inside me that propelled me to my feet in record-breaking time as I tried to catch a closer look.

Frantically I searched the shoreline with my eyes as all my senses in unison warned me to slowly back away from the dark, surging water.

"Aden?"

I jumped, physically jumped, turning to see my father standing right there behind me.

"Geez, Dad. You scared the crap out of me!"

"What? I'm sorry."

He stood there for a moment, unsure of what to say or do next. After a minute of slow, deliberate breathing, my heart rate returned to normal and I was able to then explain my sudden reaction.

"I just thought that I saw something strange out there in the water."

For a second he hesitated and I thought that he was going to ask me to describe what exactly I had seen, but just as quickly he dismissed it.

"You're probably just a little nervous about your trip tomorrow. I spoke to your aunt earlier. She said she already has your room ready to go and is really excited to see you again. She told me that she is looking forward to spending some quality time with her favorite nephew."

"I'm her only nephew," I replied dryly, rolling my eyes.

With a slight frown on his face my father asked, "How was the party? How's Abby?"

I noticed the way he drawled out his last question.

"Dad! We're just friends!"

"I know, but I can also tell that she likes you."

"Well it doesn't matter anymore, does it?!" I said, just a little too harshly.

Immediately I began to feel bad. I didn't want to end this night arguing with my father. This was the last night that we would be together for who knew how long. I was leaving tomorrow morning and he would be getting on a boat soon in October, staying gone at sea for four long months, two to four weeks at a time. Besides, he had already promised me that if I hated my new school, I could come back after January and finish up my second semester here.

"I'm sorry," I apologized to him quietly.

"Here. Come sit beside me," he said.

He lowered himself onto the ground and gestured to a rocky spot on the beach to his left. Obediently, I followed suit.

"I've been wanting to have this talk with you for quite some time now," he said. "I wanted to tell you not to be afraid of love just because of what happened to me. I loved your mother with all of my heart and if I had known then how it would end, I would have done everything the same all over again. You know what they say, 'It's better to have loved and lost...'"

"'Than to have never loved at all,'" I finished the quote thoughtfully.

Taking a deep breath, I knew that he was right.

"I promise you, Dad, from now on I will be more open to the possibility," I said, suddenly sounding more optimistic than I felt inside.

"Good! Now I also have a couple of things to give you before you go."

He turned and pulled out a little black book with my name engraved on the bottom of the cover on the right hand side.

"A Bible?" I asked.

"It's from your grandmother. She also told me to remind you to say your prayers every night before you go to bed," he said with a smile.

Coming from five generations of southern Baptists, we had been required, by grandmother's law, to go to the tiny white church on the hill every Sunday morning and Wednesday night, come hell or high water. I could feel myself smiling, imagining my dear grandmother speaking the words of my father's message.

The next choice of words that my father spoke were no longer lighthearted. The tone of his voice had dropped and his mood suddenly became very serious.

"The other thing I have for you is a gift from your mother. I wasn't supposed to give it to you until next year because she had left it in your baby basket, along with a note that said she wanted it to be your eighteenth birthday present. However, I decided that since you are leaving, I thought you might want to go ahead and take it with you now."

From the inside of a brown leather pouch he pulled out a black, leather cord necklace that held a white, luminous stone. The moon made it shimmer with an almost magical iridescence and I could see the inscription of a silver arrow in the middle.

"Wow!" I said staring at it in wonder.

"It's a Moonstone," he told me, "also called a Dream Stone. It is said to bring the one who wears it lovely visions at night… you know, sweet dreams."

"It's really cool Dad, but do you know what's with the arrow?"

I could see his face begin to contort as he contemplated the answer.

"I'm not really sure. Your mother went hunting with me a lot. She was really good with the bow, like you. Maybe she was just hoping that you would enjoy the sport as well. I wish that she was here to see you now," he added, stifling a laugh and stuffing the necklace back into the pouch before handing it over to me.

I could feel my father's mood begin to shift and decided that I'd better quickly change the subject.

"Do you think that I should gather a few of these agates for Aunt Tess? You know how much she likes to collect different types of stones."

Tons of them had washed ashore, littering the beach, after the nearby volcano Redoubt had erupted several years ago.

"I think that she would like that," he replied thoughtfully.

After a moment of silence he stood up, helping me to my feet.

"It's getting late. I think that we should be heading home. You've got an early flight to catch."

He put his arm around me as we walked toward the little cabin we called home. I decided now was the time to tell my father something that I had wanted to say to him for quite some time now.

"Thank you, dad."

"For what, son?"

"Everything. The advice, the gifts, everything you have done and sacrificed in the past to raise me."

He stopped, turning to wrap me in his big strong arms, just like he had when I was a little boy. Instantly I felt that familiar sense of safety, knowing without a doubt that he would lay down his life to protect mine.

"I did the best I could."

"You did good, Dad. Promise me that you will be careful out there on the boat without me to take care of you."

"I promise," he whispered, and as he pulled away, I thought I saw the glint of a tear in his eye.

Melissa watched longingly as Brogan and Aden made their way back to the quaint, cozy cabin. These were the two people that she loved the most in this world, but could no longer be with. She had made the decision long ago to give them up and had done her best to stay away. It was for their own good.

There were times like this, in a moment of weakness, when she would come back around, taking care to keep herself hidden, just to feel close to them. The years had been kind to Brogan, making him only seem all the more attractive to her now. Looking at Aden, she could hardly believe that her little baby was now almost a man.

What she wouldn't give if she could just hold them one more time. Tell them that she loved them. Wish her son a Happy Birthday.

It just didn't seem fair.

How easy it would be to go knock on that door. Apologize for everything. Just start over. The brightness of this thought quickly faded as the thought of her responsibilities and what would then happen sharply brought her back to reality.

"Watch over him," Melissa whispered to her companion. "Make sure that he is safe while he is away from his father."

"I always do. What about the necklace?"

"*Let him keep it. There's only one more year left until he turns eighteen. I don't think that it could hurt anything.*"

After her companion nodded in agreement, Melissa turned back to look at the cabin door. With one last glance at the life she could have had, Melissa turned, forcing herself to move away from her spot alongside the edge of the cloud, high above the little cabin.

Chapter 2

New Waters

I watched through the window as the plane made its descent into Tampa's International Airport. It was 6:00pm Eastern time now and I'd been up for the past twelve hours catching planes from Kenai, to Anchorage, to Los Angeles and then, finally, to Tampa. From here it would be another forty-five minute drive south to my new home, located on Anna Maria Island.

Drowsily I thought about the last time that I had been here. I was seven, so it must have been about ten years earlier. Tess had just moved down here from Alaska to be with her new boyfriend Greg, whom she had met on the internet. It was that summer that I had come to visit her.

Fondly, I remembered Greg. He had worked nearby for the U.S. Fish and Wildlife Service at the Egmont Key National Wildlife Refuge, which I thought had to be the coolest job ever. Knowing my love for animals, he had planned a trip to the island, then taken us all out on a boat, which was the only way we could get to Egmont Key from the mainland. There we saw sting-rays, dolphins, manatees, fish and lots of other fascinating creatures of the sea.

My fondest memory of the trip was going out to the beach one night when the moon was full and seeing several sea turtles come up onto the beach to lay their eggs. I remembered Alana and I had pretended to be spies, dressed all in black with our flashlights illuminated red. Greg had told us that this was necessary so we wouldn't scare the turtles or disturb their nesting process. Once the turtles had begun to lay their eggs, he told us that it was safe to cautiously approach them.

Once they were finished and headed back toward the sea, we actually got to touch them. He let us rub their backs and we watched in amazement as they began to glow lime green. He taught us that it was the bioluminescent algae that grew on their shells which caused the strange, other worldly illumination.

I wished that Greg would be here now. However, last I heard my Aunt was dating a new guy, some hot shot lawyer who lived nearby in Bradenton.

When the plane landed, I was the first one off. After so many hours in the air I couldn't wait to be back on solid ground. I grabbed my guitar case and quickly made my way from the gate, down through the terminal to the baggage claim.

I found my old, worn out navy duffle bag on the baggage carousel right away and then began to search for my aunt in the crowd of people. After only a moment, I spotted a teenage girl holding a sign with my name on it. As I walked closer, I recognized that it was actually my cousin, all grown up.

Alana's curly auburn hair hung past her shoulders with a few streaks of black framing her face. She had on a fitted white tank top that was cropped, showing off her golden belly ring. A long brown skirt that flowed to her ankles completed the look. Nervously, she played with her layered, colorful beaded necklaces while she slowly scanned the crowd. Her dark green eyes lit up when they finally met mine and she quicky rushed over to meet me.

"Hi, Aden! How was your trip?"

"Long!" I groaned, "but not too bad. Where's Aunt Tess?"

"She was unable to take off work at her shop, so you are stuck with me instead."

"Could be worse," I said smiling, as I pulled her in for a big hug.

As we walked out to the parking lot, I noticed that Alana had a large tattoo of a vibrant tiger lily on the back of her right shoulder blade. On top of the colorful flower sat a small, pretty fairy with long brown hair and a wispy orange dress. The details were so intricate and the image so lifelike, I could have sworn the little pixie had just winked at me.

We stopped beside a beautiful 1957 arctic blue Corvette convertible. It had been refurbished with 19" chrome wheels and white leather seats. It reminded me of the vintage cars that I would see every year when my father took me up to Anchorage for Shine and Show, the famous annual car show.

"This is us," Alana said.

Unable to control my excitement, I blurted out, "No way! This car's awesome! Is it yours?"

Alana laughed.

"No. It's my mom's. A present from Chad."

Must be her new boyfriend's name, I thought to myself as I tossed my things into the back and stood alongside the passenger door. I looked longingly over at the ignition.

"Can I drive?" I asked with enthusiasm, shaking my head yes, in hopes that she would just go along with it.

She rolled her eyes before casually replying, "Not a chance," then slid in behind the wheel.

We navigated our way from the airport parking lot out onto

the highway. With the top down, the ride to the house was invigorating. The weather was perfect and the sun was low on the horizon, now only about an hour from setting. It was much warmer than I was used to in Alaska, so I found myself taking off my boots and stripping down to my undershirt and jeans.

Alana pulled her sunglasses down her nose and looked over at me.

"I'll take you shopping tomorrow for some cooler clothes."

"Thanks. I think I'm gonna need some shades too. Everything is so much brighter here."

She must have found my comment funny, because I saw her try to hide a smile as she pushed her glasses back into place, glancing back at the road.

My dad had given me what little bit of money he had to help with my clothing expenses. We figured that my summer clothes might work for the winter time here, but I really didn't have a whole lot that I would be able to wear till then. He said that he would send me more once he got his first paycheck from his new job, but that wouldn't be until October and today was only July twenty-second.

I thought to myself that maybe I should try to get a job.

We drove through St. Petersburg and headed toward Bradenton on I-275 over the Sunshine Skyway Bridge. To my left was Tampa Bay and on my right the Gulf waters glittered golden in the setting sunlight. I looked down as we topped the crest of the bridge to watch a large cruise ship sail underneath us, heading out toward the open ocean. All of the people on board were looking up, waving and smiling with little umbrella drinks in their hands. They all seemed so happy and relaxed, ready to enjoy their vacation and begin a new adventure.

"We're really high," I said, turning back around in my seat.

"One hundred and ninety-three feet at the highest point," Alana told me matter-of-factly.

As the wind blew through my hair, I leaned back to enjoy the view on what was left of this amazing ride. I could easily get used to this, I thought to myself.

By the time we pulled in through the wrought iron gate of my aunt's home, it was already beginning to get dark. This was definitely not the house I remembered from my childhood.

The lights were on inside the large three-story Mediterranean style home with white stucco walls and a terra cotta tile roof. A large archway with a decorative keystone welcomed visitors at the entrance and several smaller arches covered large balconies on the upper levels. A silver Honda sat in the driveway.

"The Civic is mine." Alana told me. "Mom thought that you would enjoy the view better in the convertible, so she took my car to work with her this morning."

I nodded in appreciation.

As we walked up the stairs, Tess flung open the doors and rushed out to meet us. Her fine, wavy hair was the same auburn color as Alana's, with just a few streaks of grey throughout. Her eyes were the same warm, dark brown as my father's.

"Aden! You have most certainly grown up since the last time I saw you. My, haven't you gotten handsome."

I blushed as she gave me a warm hug and a quick kiss on the cheek.

"I brought you some agates that I gathered on the beach to add to your collection," I told her as I handed her the small leather pouch that I had pulled from my bag.

"Oh, my! You're so thoughtful, too. How sweet! You should probably keep one for yourself, though. You know they say agates have the power to calm fevers, quench thirst and divert storms."

"No, I didn't know that."

"Yes, and the stone that you wear around your neck…"

"Moonstone. I know that one. My father told me."

"Correct! It brings sweet dreams and strengthens your emotional and subconscious aspects. I remember long ago seeing that necklace on your mother. She was so stunning. It was no wonder that your father was so smitten with her."

"You knew my mother?!!"

"Well, I only met her once. I'll tell you more about that story later. Right now I'm running late to meet Chad for dinner. I ordered you guys a pizza. It's staying warm in the microwave. Alana will help you find your room and get you settled in. Be good and I will see you guys later."

With another quick hug and kiss, she took the keys from Alana, started up the 'Vette and backed out the driveway.

I looked over at my cousin. She must have read the questions in my eyes, for she said, "Get used to it. She's never here. She spends almost every night at Chad's house and during the day she has her candle shop down in Sarasota to tend to. You'll hardly ever see her."

With a sigh she added, "Come on, let's get you inside."

I walked through the front entry way into the living room and the first thing I noticed was a broom, brushy side up, sitting right beside the door. My attention was quickly diverted to the walls which were hard to miss as they were so brightly colored. The decor was done in a modern, eclectic style.

I noticed several different table cloths, set up on small tables in the far corner to my right. Each one was a different color. One was purple, one gold and the other a dusty rose. They each had different artifacts, pictures, candles, gemstones and other oddities placed in careful formations on top of them.

Taking a deep breath, I could smell a lingering scent of lavender and rose incense. It seemed to have been recently burnt.

"What are those?" I asked, gesturing to the colorful, intricately detailed displays.

"Those are Pagan altars."

"Pagan? What does that mean?"

"It's a form of religion, with a connection to and a reverence for nature. It's a branch of Polytheism."

I looked at her like she had just spoken Japanese.

With a little less patience she continued to explain. "It basically means that instead of worshiping one God like you do with Christianity, we worship multiple deities. We believe that there are many different gods and goddesses who take care of different aspects of the universe. You know like the sun, the moon, the earth, the seas and so on. We build these altars as a place to worship, to pray to the gods of our choice."

She led me over to the gold table.

"For example, here we pray for wealth. At the rose table we pray for love, and at the purple table we pray for help to ease our fear and anxiety."

I couldn't believe what I was hearing.

"That seems ridiculous!" I scoffed with a little laugh.

She stepped back and looked offended for a moment before coming right back at me, "Don't be so closed minded, Aden!

Just because it's not what *you* believe, how *you* were raised. Lots of people believe the exact same thing, like the Hindus and the Native Americans. How would you like to make it to the gates of heaven and find Buddha sitting there guarding the entrance?"

I started to feel bad that I had just angered her so easily.

"Okay," I said, "you've made your point. I'm sorry."

I saw her take a deep breath, trying to calm herself.

"It's all right," she said. "I was just trying to say that you shouldn't be so quick to judge someone else's beliefs. What's really important is that you believe in something. Right?"

"Well I guess so," I muttered, still slightly confused.

Alana turned toward the stairs and started up them before yelling back to me, "Are you ready to go see your new room?"

Welcoming the change of topic, I followed her up to the second floor. At the end of the hall she opened the door then held it open so that I could enter.

The room was large with a light tan carpet. The ceiling had been painted black and three of the walls were covered in a deep navy blue. On the fourth wall, someone had painted a mural of a dense forest with a mountain range in the background that went all the way up to the ceiling.

"I designed it to remind you of being home in Alaska," Alana said. "I hope that you like it."

"It's amazing!" I uttered.

Suddenly I felt overwhelmed by the effort that she had put into making me feel so welcome.

"Thank you very much!"

She gestured toward the big black comforter that had been spread on top of a full sized bed and plopped herself down onto it.

"Come. Lay down for a second."

I threw my bag on the floor then jumped up to join her on the cozy, plush bed. She clapped twice and the overhead lights went out.

"Look. I did the stars for you, too."

I looked up and saw dozens of glowing stars all over the dark ceiling. They had been placed carefully in the form of different constellations.

"I used a map of the night sky to figure out the placements," she said, "and I made sure that all of the constellations were accounted for. See, there's Orion's Belt, the Big Dipper, Little Dipper, the Archer, even the Crab, which represents Cancer, your zodiac sign. They're all up there."

I saw her look over at me, eagerly awaiting my reaction. Even though the outside light coming through the window was extremely dim, I knew she could tell that I was smiling.

"Way cool. That was so thoughtful, Alana. You really didn't have to go through all of this trouble."

I looked over and saw her smiling back at me.

"I know," she said. "I've just been really excited ever since I found out that you were coming to live here. I spend a lot of time in this house all alone and now it will be like I have a little brother to take care of."

She clapped again and the lights came back on.

"I'm only a few months younger than you," I said, "and if you haven't noticed, I'm not that little."

"It doesn't matter," she said, sitting up and playfully punching me on the arm. "I'll still end up having to take care of you."

She got up and walked around, enthusiastically pulling me up off the bed.

"Come take a look at the view from your balcony," she said.

I stepped outside into the warm, humid twilight. The sun had already set, but there was still just enough light to see the ocean view from one side of my balcony. The sky was a faint orange with pink and purple clouds drifting lazily over the calm water. The island we were on was small enough that if I looked out from the other side of the balcony, I could see a clear view of the tranquil bay that separated us from the mainland.

I plopped down in one of the welcoming, oversized lounge chairs. I was in awe how peaceful this place was.

Strange. Just this morning I had been dreading the move here, but now that I had made it, I had the funny feeling that this was exactly the place that I was supposed to be.

I closed my eyes and began to feel the effects of my extremely long day. Alana's voice brought me back from the brink of an unplanned slumber.

"I'll leave you alone so that you can settle in and unpack," she said. "We still have a few weeks before school starts, so I'll be able to show you around so you can get better acquainted with the island."

Every muscle in my body protested as I lifted myself off the cushy chair. I followed Alana back inside to the cool air-conditioned room and before she left, I managed to utter my thanks once again.

The moment she shut the door, I crawled back into the comfortable bed, still in my undershirt and jeans. The jersey cotton sheets felt so cozy and I was so completely exhausted, that I was immediately swallowed by the darkness of a deep dreamless sleep.

Nitra came through her mother's bedroom door with her head hanging down, fully prepared to face her mother's wrath as she relayed the bad news. Touching her mother's arm, she spoke in a low regretful voice.

"I lost him."

Vanessa's words seethed with anger. "What do you mean you lost him? I just saw you watching him last night."

Using the gift that her brother Adrian had given her, Vanessa had been able to watch through it as her daughter attempted to sneak up to the rocky beach that the boy had been sitting on. She couldn't be sure, but it almost seemed as if he had somehow sensed her daughter's arrival.

Nitra continued to try to explain meekly, "Something about the whole situation just didn't feel right."

She could feel the tension as her mother's heated gaze penetrated through her skin.

"I asked you to do one simple task," Vanessa told her daughter. "Was it because of his father showing up? You could have just taken them both down. I know the horrors that you are capable of."

"I was going to, but because of the odd feeling that I was getting, I decided that it was best to wait and come back in the morning. The problem was when I got to the cabin this morning, he was already gone, along with all of his things."

Vanessa wanted to scream because of her daughter's incompetence. They had been so close!

"Go back!" she said seething . "Go into the town if you have to. Find him! Question everyone. We must find him no matter what. Use whatever means necessary!"

Chapter 3

Enchanted

The end of the summer came much too quickly. Surprisingly, the last few weeks I'd spent with my cousin hadn't been half bad. Not bad at all really. I found myself actually enjoying her company and had even gotten used to some of her endearing quirkiness.

I still missed my dad of course, but we'd kept in touch with frequent phone calls and sporadic emails. Besides, with my Aunt gone all the time, Alana and I basically got to do whatever we wanted, whenever we wanted to. The freedom made the time we spent together all the more fun.

In the past couple of weeks, Alana had taken me fishing at several of the local hot spots. This included the Anna Maria City Pier, where we'd run into a couple of her guy friends. I remembered sitting there on the wooden planks with my legs dangling over the edge as they walked up. I was holding my fishing pole, looking up, waiting for her to introduce me, but she never did. I watched for a moment, completely forgotten, as she became awkwardly nervous in her attempt to flirt with the taller one with the shaggy brown hair.

Turning back to the water amused, I tried to pretend that I wasn't listening to them. After several minutes of small talk, the lanky dude began to dominate the conversation. The longer he and Alana talked, or should I say he talked, in his obviously fake Australian accent, the less I could figure out what exactly it was that she saw in this guy. He seemed like a complete narcissist to me.

After they finally left, Alana seemed to suddenly remember that I was still sitting there. Apologizing, she quickly told me a little bit about who they were. I learned they were both football players from my soon-to-be high school. Jason, the one that she had a crush on was a running back and Zach, who played safety, dated some cheerleader named Leslie.

Alana and I, over the past few weeks, had eaten at almost all of the local restaurants. Never the same one twice. Alana had then lectured me about the importance of expanding my palate, knowing all the different types of cuisine that the island had to offer. She said it would help me to feel more at home and less like a tourist. She also more recently admitted that the reason we always ate out was because she was a complete disaster in the kitchen.

The beach had been another place that we hung out frequently, at her insistence. I could still hear her annoyingly bossy voice in my head.

"I refuse to be seen with you in public if your skin remains that pale, pasty yellow," she only half-joked.

Not that I really cared, but I did have to admit that I looked much better now, much healthier, since my skin had become a nice golden bronze. Now it actually looked like it absorbed the sunlight instead of reflecting it.

We had also been to the mall here in Bradenton, where Alana had taken me shopping and bought me tons of shorts, T-shirts and flip-flops. "The unofficial uniform of guys here in Florida," her words exactly.

The best thing of all was that I hadn't even had to spend

any of my own money yet. Aunt Tess had given me several hundred dollar bills to spend on clothes and school supplies and she was now giving Alana and I both a generous allowance every week. I figured she might be feeling a little bit guilty about all the time that she spent away.

As we pulled up to the school in the Civic for our first day, I pulled down my new polarized Costas and surveyed the place that I would now be spending most of my days. It was a huge, two-story, red brick building with six large white columns that held up a Grecian portico in the front. In deep red letters, etched onto the front were the words "Manatee High School."

The entrance jutted out about ten feet from the rest of the building and was flanked on either side by single palm trees, each one taller than the building itself. An American flag flew proudly, high up on a white flag pole protruding from a perfectly landscaped island in the middle of the front walkway.

Because the school was located on the mainland in Bradenton, not Anna Maria Island, it was much larger than I had anticipated. With all the brick and ancient architecture, I thought that it looked more like a courthouse than a school.

Alana walked with me through the front double doors to the office, where we met with the secretary and picked up our schedules for the first semester. When we compared them, we found that we only had one class together, third period, Physics. Bummer. I had really been hoping that we would have more, since she was the only person that I really knew here at this school. I groaned internally at the thought of having to start all over, making new friends. Breathing deeply, I decided just to try and make the best of it.

As we began to walk down the hall, I noticed that everyone was staring at us. It started to make me feel slightly uncomfortable, so I decided just to focus on reading some of the red and blue banners that were hanging everywhere in the hall. Most of them attempted to evoke school spirit with the words "MHS Hurricanes" or "Go Canes!" Others advertised different school clubs and activities. There were even a few that issued a welcoming invitation to the incoming freshmen.

I walked Alana to her Calculus class, which was the same room that I would spend my fourth period in. She then pointed me down the hall just a little further, toward the gym.

My very first class was Physical Education and I was kicking myself for not thinking to bring tennis shoes to change into. I definitely wouldn't be able to run in these fashionably tattered, brown flip-flops. The last few students that remained in the hall rushed into the doors of their classrooms just as the bell suddenly rang.

Great! I thought. Late on my first day!

I slowed my pace to give myself time to think about exactly what I was going to say to the coach.

Suddenly I heard a sweet, soft voice begin to sing. I stopped in my tracks, trying to locate the source of this unexpected serenade. It sounded like it was coming from one of the open doors, just ahead of me.

The melody was melancholic and haunting, yet hypnotically intriguing. I recognized the tune but couldn't think of the name of the song, not when it was the voice that had me completely enchanted. Nothing existed in this moment except for the voice. It was intoxicating and refreshing, rapturous and otherworldly. It made me completely forget where I had just been headed to, only a moment ago.

I felt a cool tingling, like a low volt of electricity. It flooded throughout my entire body, giving me the strangest calming sensation, making my legs feel like Jell-O. The music grew louder and I was drawn like a moth to a flame toward the door on my right, which had been left ajar.

There was no fighting it. I had to see for myself the host of this young female voice that sounded so ethereal. I half expected to see an angel singing as I walked through the entrance of the door labeled Music Room.

The first thing I noticed about her was her large, turquoise eyes. They were locked on mine, waiting for my entry as if she had known that I was coming. Her eyes were so stunning, with a stare so intense, that I had to stop in my tracks just to catch my breath. I tried to smile or to move. I tried to do anything, but it felt as if every single muscle in my body was paralyzed, refusing to function.

I was truly entranced.

Out of my peripheral vision I could see that the classroom, which was set up like an auditorium, was full of other students whose gaze fell intently on her as well. Because the door was to their backs and they too seemed mesmerized by her song, no one else even noticed me come in.

Her appearance matched her angelic voice. Beyond beautiful, she had on a white linen dress that ruffled in the light cool breeze that was coming from the air-conditioner vents. Long, golden blonde hair fell in loose waves that were layered to her waist. Her smooth, flawless skin had a lovely hue that seemed to glow in the overhead florescent lighting and I noticed that her silver and turquoise jewelry matched the color of her eyes precisely.

I stood in the doorway as she continued to sing, both of us still staring at the other. My mind told me that I should probably try to look away, but my body protested at the impossible task. Her stare softened with the slightest of a smile and I could feel my frigid heart begin to melt.

After the song had come to an end, a man's squeaky voice snapped me out of my trance. He was short and wore a horribly obvious toupee on his balding head.

"Excuse me! Young man, what is your name?"

Everyone looked back to the door to see who their teacher was talking to.

"A-Aden, Aden Wilder," I managed to stutter.

"Well, Mr. Wilder, I know this is not the classroom you are supposed to be in, because all of my students are present and accounted for. You have just interrupted our preliminary auditions so unless you would like to get up on the stage and entertain us, I suggest you go find your original destination before I am forced to send you to the principal's office."

I turned around, quickly embarrassed by his pointed words and harsh tone.

He's such a jerk, I thought. I wanted to go knock that stupid piece of fur off his stupid, ugly head.

I walked down the hall in a huff to the gymnasium, which was closer and much quieter than I had expected. After I entered through the double doors, I quickly figured out why. The whole place was empty. Backpacks and shoes cluttered the far bleachers, but all the seats were unoccupied.

Listening to far away voices and laughter, I followed their

sound to the back door of the gym that had been left propped open. I saw a small field at the side of the building where the class had already assembled. They were playing a game of kick ball.

As I walked down from the covered, concrete pathway onto the foot-worn trail and out into the sunshine, I began to realize how ridiculously hot it was today. The only relief was an occasional warm tropical breeze that blew in from the gulf.

I saw the coach standing over on the sidelines and walked straight to her to introduce myself, apologizing for my unplanned tardiness. Coach Hall was a pretty, petite lady who, luckily, was very nice too. She had her hair neatly pulled back, tucked under a Manatee County baseball cap, and wore a matching red polo that read "Staff". There was a large, yellow plastic whistle that hung loosely around her neck. She told me that she could understand my tardiness, with it being my first day and could see how I might not know yet what I needed to bring with me. She said that I could just sit on the bleachers and watch for today.

I climbed up the stairs to the top of the rickety, portable metal bleachers and sat beside an athletic looking guy wearing loose red basketball shorts. He had a deep, dark tan and short black hair.

"Hi, I'm Michael," he said, turning to me and shaking my hand.

When I told him who I was and said my last name, he asked if I was Alana's cousin and I nodded yes. He quickly told me that he was a friend of Alana's and that she had mentioned before that I would be coming.

Happy to now know someone, I sat back and tried to enjoy

the game, but all I could think about was how I wished that I was in music class instead. I could play the guitar, so maybe there was a chance that I could audition late. Then I thought about how unfriendly the music teacher had been. Auditioning seemed doubtful.

Bringing myself back into the moment I noticed the team kicking was on it's final out and the bases were loaded. At first I thought it was my imagination and if it hadn't been for the cool tingling I began to feel again, this time less intensely, I might have dismissed it as wishful thinking. Amazingly, the girl on third base looked almost identical to the angel that was in the music room.

There were subtle differences though. Her hair was a darker blonde and it was French braided across the front, pulled back into a low ponytail with a pink ribbon that matched her tank top, fingernails, lip gloss and shoes. The only thing she was wearing that wasn't pink was her skimpy black athletic shorts. Her skin was a much paler ivory and when she turned to look at me, I noticed her heavily made-up eyes were a deeper blue.

The game resumed when a guy with sandy blonde hair that was spiked in the front, kicked the ball so hard that it sailed through the air to the very back of the field before rolling into the woods.

Ever so gracefully, Pinkie danced her way to home plate, where she stood giving high fives to the other two players that followed her in. The guy who kicked the grand slam effortlessly ran the bases so quickly that he arrived on home plate just after the guy who was in front of him. His athletic body was long and lean and he was wearing pants, which I thought was crazy considering the intense heat. However, his skin showed no hint of perspiration. Standing beside the girl in pink I could see that his skin was the same pale shade of ivory as hers.

After he touched the base, the girl in pink reached up on her tiptoes and gave him a quick kiss on the lips. I then I saw her whisper something into his ear. When he looked up, his hazel-green eyes met mine for just a split second. With a quick nod, he then looked away and went back to working the cheering crowd.

Weird, I thought to myself.

I watched them both go back to the other set of bleachers and have a drink from matching sports bottles. After making sure they weren't looking my way, I decided to ask Michael some questions about the strange couple.

"Who's the guy that just scored the slam?"

"Oh, that's Liam Garrett. He's the quarterback of our football team. He also wrestles and plays on the golf and basketball teams."

Now I could ask the question I really wanted to know.

"What about the girl?"

"His girlfriend. Her name is Katiana, but everyone calls her Kat. They've been together ever since they moved here freshman year."

"They moved here at the same time?"

"Well, actually no. Liam started that fall, but Kat didn't show up till later on that spring."

"Does Kat happen to have a sister?"

"Yeah, a twin actually. We call them the Jensen twins. Her name is Kailani but she prefers to be called Kaili. She's a little more quiet and reserved than Kat is."

Kailani. I tested the name out with my tongue. What an unusual, yet beautiful name it seemed to me.

Trying to sound simply curious, I asked "Does Kailani have a boyfriend too?"

Michael laughed just a little before saying, "No. Don't even bother wasting your time man. Kaili doesn't date."

My next few classes flew by, Government, then Physics, followed by the dreaded Calculus. I was finding it impossible to concentrate on my subjects though, as my thoughts kept returning to the gorgeous blond with the turquoise eyes, Kailani.

The jarring sound of the bell dismissing us for lunch startled me out of my thoughts and I went to my locker to meet Alana before heading into the cafeteria. After waiting in line for ten minutes to purchase the mystery burritos that they called "fish tacos", we went to go find a seat.

I recognized the guy from the pier, Jason, as he waved Alana and I over to sit in the two seats that he'd reserved for us at his table. Michael was there too, sitting beside him on the very end. I took the seat directly across from Michael so that Alana could sit in front of Jason. On his other side, I recognized the other guy from the pier that day, Zach. I assumed the girl with the long dark hair sitting beside him was his girlfriend, Leslie. In front of her there were a couple of girls that I had never met before.

I noticed the tingling sensation had returned and when I looked down to the far end of the table, my heart skipped a beat. There was Liam and Kat and I could tell that Kailani was sitting across from her sister, even though I couldn't see her very well. There were several people between us that were blocking my view. I did notice that she had the same matching sports bottle next to her lunch tray as the others that I'd seen earlier. They were metal and opaque so I couldn't be sure what was inside.

I was startled to realize that here, in the cool cafeteria, Kat was not nearly as pale as I had originally thought. In fact, she was the exact same hue of medium beige as her sister. Liam even looked slightly darker. I thought maybe it had just been a trick of the light that I'd noticed out there in the bright sunshine.

My heart started hammering in my chest and I could still feel that now familiar cool prickling of my skin, but luckily, this time, none of them were looking my way. I turned toward Alana, so that I could peek in their direction every once in a while without being so obvious.

My delightful cousin then took it upon herself to start introducing me to everyone. She started with Michael then worked her way clockwise around the table. When she said Liam and Kat's name, they smiled at me and waved, as the others had. Kailani, however, only looked at me for a split second, nodded her head, then looked over at Kat before turning to play with her food.

Out of the corner of my eye I saw a bleached blond girl walk up and stand right beside me. Her hair was cut short, shaved in the back with the front pieces straightened down to her jaw line. She had on a white miniskirt with a tight, low-cut black top and wore over-sized silver hoop earrings.

"Dang, Alana!" she said, "You told me that your cousin was coming to join us for our senior year, but you forgot to mention that he was a T-total hottie!"

As she spoke, she ran her hand down my shoulder then held it out for me to shake.

"Hi, I'm Brooke."

"Aden, nice to meet . . ."

"Nobody cares, Brooke," interrupted Michael. "Go sit down."

"Jealous?" she responded, sticking her tongue out in a childish gesture.

She tapped Alana on the shoulder, signaling for her to move over. Despite giving Alana my best "do it and you die" look, she scooted down into the empty chair beside her. As Brooke then took her seat, I glared at my cousin over her shoulder.

Throughout the rest of the lunch break, Brooke was turned toward me, giggling whenever I said something, batting her eyelashes and asking me all kinds of questions about myself. The only time she ever stopped was when Michael would make a snide comment or call her a name. She would respond with quick quips, just as childish and then turn her attention right back to me.

I guess in a way she was pretty, but I was still having trouble concentrating on anything but the beautiful girl behind her, sitting at the other end of the table. Whenever I could, I would steal a glimpse of her.

Everyone else was talking back and forth to each other, except for Kailani, she was silent. Occasionally, Kat would look over at her sister, then briefly direct her attention my way.

When the bell rang to signal the end of lunch, everyone started to get up and head back to class. Amidst the commotion,

I felt a sudden breeze rustle through the cafeteria and Brooke's red fruit juice then tipped over, spilling into her lap and all over her bright white skirt.

As she screamed, now distracted, I looked behind her trying to catch one more glimpse at the object of my new, unexplainable obsession. Someone was standing in the way, so for a brief moment Kat caught my attention. She was gazing over at her sister with raised eyebrows, unblinking. When the person in front of me moved I saw Kailani was staring right back at her.

Obviously Kailani had found the little incident amusing because I saw a hint of a smile lift one side of her lip, but just as quickly it was gone.

She stood to leave, her face now passive, and completely ignored the hysterical girl sobbing something about her new Ralph Lauren now being completely ruined.

Chapter 4

Lucky

After lunch, the next class on my schedule was Art, which was normally one of my favorites and something I was really good at. The teacher had set up the desks to form tables so that we were all facing one another in groups of four. I supposed the design was meant to stimulate our social creativity.

When I walked over to the window in the back of the room, I recognized the faces of a couple of the girls from the lunch table and they raised their hands, waving to indicate that I was welcome to come sit with them. Alana had introduced us earlier, but with all the distractions, I couldn't remember their names. Thankfully, Destiny and Arianna repeated them as I sat down. They were both very welcoming with easy, cheerful dispositions. As they continued to talk, I couldn't help but think about how friendly all of the girls here in Florida had been to me.

Well, all except for one.

Because it was our first day Mrs. Mallory, my Art teacher, didn't ask us to create anything or start any new projects. Instead, she put on a slide show and gave us a brief introduction to Art History. She then went through the syllabus to familiarize us with some of the things that we would be covering in our lessons the rest of this semester. Tomorrow, we would begin with painting in watercolors.

My last class of the day was World Literature. I walked

in scanning the room, hoping to see Kailani, praying that we would have at least one class together. It had been like this all day. Every time I would enter another classroom, the hope and anticipation would grip me, just as if it was a physical being. I thought to myself, "This will be my last chance."

Unfortunately she wasn't here either. Instead, I saw Brooke, who frantically waved me over, motioning for me to come and sit at the desk in front of hers. Obligingly, I threw my backpack onto the floor and slid into the plastic chair behind the wooden workspace. Brooke placed her hand on my shoulder and started to say something, when Michael took the seat beside me, greeting me with a fist bump. He was ranting excitedly about how the day was almost over, which I could tell obviously agitated Brooke because of the fact that he had stolen my attention away from her.

As luck would have it, just before the bell rang, I felt that cool, tingling sensation that proceeded Kailani as she walked through the classroom door. Anxiously I looked up and immediately her eyes met mine. This time she smiled, bigger than before, as she came to sit in the last available seat, right in front of mine. What luck!

She turned around, looking at me with those unbelievable turquoise eyes. Up close, they reminded me of looking into a pool, so clear and inviting that I would willingly jump right in. I knew I could happily spend an eternity there, easily losing myself in the crisp, clean water.

When she spoke, it was with the same soft, musical quality that I'd heard before in her voice. It was soothing, warm and endearing. The words that came from her mouth sounded just as smooth as silk.

"I'm sorry about this morning," she said, then paused, obviously expecting a response.

All she received though was my dumbfounded expression. I couldn't possibly fathom what she could have possibly done that she felt the need to apologize for.

"You know, Logan…I mean Mr. Spencer, he isn't normally like that. He must have just been having a bad day."

I wanted to say something, anything, just to hear her speak again, but unfortunately at that very moment our teacher decided to begin his class and I only got in a quick nod before she turned back around in her seat.

"Hello class! My name is Mr. Mitchell and I will be your World Literature teacher this year."

He was short and stocky with dark hair that was thick on the sides, but he was balding on the top. His voice was deep but still excitable at the same time.

"I am terrible with names, so to help me to remember yours. I ask that you each remain in these same seats for the rest of the semester. That way I can also tell who is missing, without having to do a roll call every day."

More luck, I thought. I'm going to get to stay right behind Kailani.

"This year we will be studying world myths and folktales, Shakespeare, The Iliad, Plato as well as other famous philosophers. As you are well aware, I asked each of you to read Hans Christian Andersen's delightful, yet tragic tale of 'The Little Mermaid' as your summer reading assignment."

Summer reading assignment? Oops. I had no idea.

"How many of you completed this task?"

More than half of the class raised their hands, including Kailani, though her hand rose more hesitantly than the others.

"Good. I will be giving you an oral pop quiz, starting immediately. I will ask each of you a question. If you get it correct, you will receive five extra credit points on your first test. If you get it wrong, negative five points."

"We will start with you, Anya. What year did Hans Christian Andersen write 'The Little Mermaid'?"

"1836."

"Correct! Michael, what was The Little Mermaid's name?"

"Um, Ariel?"

"No Mr. Taylor. You're thinking of the animated movie, made in 1989, based on, but slightly different from the darker, original version. Mr. Andersen actually never gave her a name. He simply referred to her as The Little Mermaid, the youngest of six sisters."

As he spoke, Mr. Mitchell paced the room, making eye contact with as many people as possible, as if he were giving a lecture. I heard Michael mumble something under his breath about being unfair and a trick question.

"Brooke, how long do the mermaids in his story typically live?"

"Approximately three hundred years," she answered smugly.

I didn't have to look at her to know that this was directed toward Michael.

"Very good! Aden?"

"Yes, sir," I replied hesitantly. Surely he didn't honestly expect me to have known about this piece of summer reading.

"I know that you are new and probably weren't aware of

this assignment, but would you care to guess what The Little Mermaid hoped to gain, besides the love of the prince, when she traded her fins for legs?"

I had no idea. I thought the only reason was love. I racked my brain. What else could a prince offer someone?

"Maybe riches?...to become a princess?"

"Sorry." His eyes were kind and his wordless smile clearly conveyed a "good try" message. His eyes left mine and he began his pacing again as he continued.

"She was already a princess. Her father was the Sea King. What she longed for the most was an immortal soul. Her grandmother told her that the only way to gain one was to marry a human. Only after they were married, and their souls joined as one, would she be able to journey to the afterlife upon her death."

He spoke with his hands, gesturing as if he were playing a game of charades, then he stopped his pacing and faced the class.

"For you see, when mermaids die they just return to the sea, simply dissolving into sea foam."

I was surprised about how sad that made me feel.

The questions continued as I stared at the back of Kailani's head. Her sunny blond hair looked so soft and luscious I had to fight the urge to reach out my hand and touch it.

"Andrew, why could The Little Mermaid not tell the prince that it was she who saved his life after the shipwreck and not the young maiden who found him on the beach?"

Andrew spoke in a low voice with his head ducked down and his eyes darting as if he were telling a scary story by the campfire.

"The witch had cut out her tongue," he said, "as payment for the draught that turned her into a human."

At the word tongue he had sliced at his own with his finger, making most of the class laugh.

After rolling his eyes, Mr. Mitchell continued with the questions, "Correct. Kate, when did the witch tell The Little Mermaid that she would die if she could not convince the prince to fall in love with and marry her?"

"The morning after he married another."

"Very good! Mila, when her sisters went to the sea witch to try to save her life, the witch chopped off all of their hair. What did she give them in return?"

"A knife to give to their sister."

"Yes! Kailani, what was she to do with this knife in order to be able to turn back into a mermaid?"

At first she didn't answer, but then in a low, almost sad voice she said, "She had to plunge it into the prince's heart before the sun rose on his wedding night, letting the blood touch her feet."

I couldn't take my eyes off of her luminous hair, yet my heart was bleeding from the emotion I thought I heard in her voice.

"Ah, yes," Mr. Mitchell added, "but she could not do this because she still loved him so. Colin, can you tell me what happened to The Little Mermaid when the sun rose that next morning?"

"Maybe," he said hesitantly. "I was kinda confused about that part. So she jumps into the ocean, right? Then it says the 'Daughters of the Air' took pity on her and raised her up to join them so that she might earn a soul after three hundred years of good deeds."

He spoke the parts about the "Daughters of the Air" and

about her being raised up very flippantly, as if he were just saying yadda yadda.

"Who were the 'Daughters of the Air'?" he then asked, "and what the heck does that mean anyway?"

"Well, I think that part of the story has long been up for interpretation," Mr. Mitchell replied. "However, most people believe that they are spirits trapped between this world and the next, each trying to earn a soul that will then admit them into heaven."

I listened to all of the questions and answers, still somewhat distracted by the tantalizing river of honey blonde hair in front of me. I had to admit I was fascinated by how the real story was so much different and morbid than the animated classic that I had grown up with.

When the quiz ended, Mr. Mitchell let us know that the teachers had placed him in charge of the Homecoming Dance committee this year and he was looking for volunteers to help him with the planning and decorations.

I saw Kailani raise her hand. Even though dances and decorations weren't really my thing, I raised my hand as well. Anything to get to spend more time with my new dream girl. Brooke volunteered next, then Michael, as well as several of the others I'd heard answering questions, none of whose names I could remember now.

When the final bell rang, everyone sprang from their seats with renewed energy. Now that the day was over and done with, the room was abuzz with students laughing and making plans for the rest of the afternoon.

Kailani turned toward me with an inquisitive look on her face, like she was going to ask me a question.

Before she could say anything Brooke wrapped her arm around my elbow then spoke softly into my ear, "Come on, I'll walk you to your car."

Kailani glanced down at Brooke's arm, then turned around and walked right out the door. I wanted to go after her to say something, but luck was no longer on my side. Besides, I couldn't think of anything to say. After grappling with my internal struggle for a moment, I allowed Brooke to continue to escort me outside, not really listening to the incessant chatter that was coming from her mouth.

When we got to the parking lot, Alana was already there, standing by her Civic. Her stance was casual, yet forced, which meant she was obviously ready to leave.

"How was your first day?" she asked with an amused grin, glancing at Brooke, then reaching for the door handle.

"Fine. Everyone is very, accommodating," I said, stressing the last word.

I watched Brooke reach into her white, patent leather Versace bag and pull out an elegant Mont Blanc pen. She grabbed for my hand, flipped it over, then wrote down her number.

"Call me," she said with a coy smile.

With a quick wave to Alana, she then walked away.

I opened the door and jumped into the car. Alana slid into the driver's seat and looked over at me.

"Someone's making quite an impression with the ladies," she said.

"Shut up," I huffed, seriously annoyed now. I put on my sunglasses.

"I'm serious. After lunch, everyone I talked to was asking about you."

I kept looking straight ahead, not willing to play along her little game. After a few seconds of silence she put the keys into the ignition and started the car.

As we were pulling out of the parking lot, I noticed Kailani sitting in a white Jeep Wrangler staring at me from a distance. I saw her startled look when she realized that I was looking right back at her. This time I somehow managed a little smile, even a wave, but it was wasted. She'd already looked away, pretending to be busy with something in her car.

Alana saw me staring and followed my gaze to figure out what, or who, exactly I was looking at. Before I realized what she was doing, she had caught me.

"So-o." She spoke the word as if it were two syllables, slow and implicating. "I can see that you've been entranced by the Jensen twins, just like every other guy in this school," she said as we pulled out onto the main road.

"Entranced? I wouldn't say that." I tried to sound nonchalant.

"Oh, give it up, Aden. I saw the way you were just looking at her and don't think I didn't notice how you kept looking behind my head today at lunch!"

I glanced at her, keeping my face impassive so as not to incriminate myself.

"It's nothing to be ashamed of. They're both very beautiful. The girls here feel the same way about Liam. If Kat wasn't in the picture, I swear I'd..."

"Where are Kat and Liam? Why are they not with her?" I asked, grasping at a chance to change the subject.

"I'm sure Liam's probably at football practice. Kat is either at cheerleading or dance rehearsal. They're both extremely popular, involved in almost every after-school activity that we have to offer, so they stay busy. Anyways, like I was saying…"

She paused and looked pointedly at me, "All of the girls like Liam, but by now they've all realized that they don't stand a chance in hell. Liam's totally in love with Kat. They fight then break up sometimes, but we all know they'll eventually end up getting back together. It never lasts long. Kat wins all of the coveted titles here: varsity cheerleading captain, dance captain of the Sugar'Canes, Miss MHS, class President, prom princess. If she wasn't so sweet, we would all hate her."

"What about Kailani?" I didn't look at her when I asked, but I could see her glance purposefully at me from the corner of my eye. I tried to ignore that.

"Well, I don't really know her that well, but I know she prefers to be called Kaili and she's not really into all of the extra curricular activities. Sometimes she stays after school to watch her sister, but most of the time I see her going home alone. I see them all riding together in the morning, so I assume she comes back later to pick up the other two."

Even knowing my next question would negate all my previous attempts to be detached and simply quizzical, I still asked, "Where do they live?"

A huge smile spread across Alana's face as she realized that she had me figured out. "Near us, in a small cottage on the southern tip of the island, with their grandmother."

My heart surged. Near us! My luck continues!

Alana's words were now muffled by my own thoughts, but I half heard her continuing, "I found that out a couple years ago when they first arrived. Brooke made me follow them."

That snapped me out of my reverie.

"She did what? Why?"

As if she shared in my outrage, Alana rolled her eyes and sighed.

"She said she doesn't trust them," her words sounded mocking, "She says there is something strange about how perfect they are. She had me follow them home to try to prove they didn't even live in our school district. After we found out that they all lived together in the cottage, Brooke started a rumor that they were brother and sisters. Ever since that day the Jensen twins and Brooke have wanted nothing to do with each other."

She paused, continuing with a smile, as if she were telling me a secret.

"That, and Brooke blames Kailani for stealing Michael away from her."

So, Michael and Brooke used to date. I thought that explained the tension I felt between them.

"But Kaili and Michael aren't together," I said quickly. It came out a little more harshly than I expected and I hoped Alana didn't hear the possessive tone that my thoughts had recently acquired.

"I know, but Brooke says Michael started ignoring her once they moved here."

"If that were true," I ventured, "I'm sure a lot of the other girls would say the same thing about their boyfriends."

After pausing, Alana turned and said, "They do."

I thought about this for a moment then asked, "One more question. Why *do* they all live together?"

"Kat said Liam ran away from home because of a bad situation. She wouldn't elaborate any more than that. Her grandmother decided to take him in several months before the girls arrived here."

When we pulled up at the house, I looked over at Alana. Instead of cutting off the ignition and exiting the car, she simply placed her hands on her lap and turned to look at me, grinning from ear to ear.

"Do you think you'll be okay by yourself tonight?" she asked.

My eyes narrowed with suspicion.

"Sure. Why?"

Now breathless with excitement, she exclaimed, "Because... I have a date with Jason!"

Annessa grabbed the sphere, pulling herself closer. She was fretting over the image that she had just seen. This boy. He was the same one who had appeared several weeks ago out of the blue. Before that night, the screen had never shown her anyone or anything that she had not first requested. It had never happened again since.

Now here he was, attending the exact same high school as her granddaughters. Coincidence? She thought not. But who was he? She decided that she would need to monitor the situation closely. If it ever appeared that her girls were in any danger, she wouldn't hesitate to call them home.

She breathed deeply. He appeared to be harmless. For now she decided that the best thing for her to do was just to watch and wait.

Chapter 5

Empathy

If I thought it had been hot this morning...Holy Crap!

After Alana left, I decided that I would go take a dip in the ocean just to get out of the house and get some fresh air. I went upstairs to change then came back down to visit the kitchen and make myself something to eat.

I was about to sauté some onions and peppers to put on top of my Philly cheese steak sandwich when I heard a loud horn honk. It was Jason.

Alana came running down the stairs.

"Don't wait up!" she called over her shoulder, not bothering to stop in the kitchen, as she hurried out the door.

Trust me, I said to myself. I wasn't planning on it.

I peeked out the window and saw her climb up into the passenger side of an old, black Chevy pick-up truck. He had not opened the car door for her and he never even bothered to come and knock on the front door. The only thing I'd heard from him was the one loud, impatient honk, which was the only real effort that he had given to this date.

I already knew that I didn't like him, but for Alana's sake I decided that I would try to see some good in him. He sure wasn't making this any easier for me.

After they left, I grabbed a Coke out of the refrigerator and sat down to eat my sandwich while I was planning the rest of my evening. I stared down at my hand. I could call

Brooke, I thought with sarcastic amusement. Yeah, right!

Another option was taking Alana's car down to the City Pier to do some fishing. This sounded good, but then I remembered how I'd felt during the past few times I'd actually caught a fish.

It was weird, ever since I moved down here to Florida I wasn't able to enjoy fishing as much as I used to. The act itself was just as much fun, but once I had the fish in my hand, trying to remove the hook, I seemed to be getting these strange feelings of fear and anxiety.

Finally, I made up my mind. Before I headed to the beach, I would stop by the picnic area on the south side of the island. Alana had taken me there several times over the summer to feed the squirrels. I remembered the first time that we went. I had been amazed to find out how uncharacteristically friendly they were here.

Up in Alaska, fear had always kept them at a safe distance. I'd only catch glimpses of them, way up in the trees. Knowing how things were there, I couldn't say that I blamed them. With all of the hunters that were in the area, I'm sure they knew they would most likely end up as a squirrel stew.

I grabbed my sunglasses and a small duffle bag that I'd stuffed with a towel, sun screen and bread, then headed out the door. Instead of taking the car I decided I would walk. I had plenty of time and nothing to do.

There was a small convenience store on the way and I stopped in to get a bag of peanuts. Afterward, when I arrived at the picnic area, I could hear the sound of the waves crashing on the other side of the small dune that separated the trees from the beach. As I walked along the trail, I heard a rustle of leaves that let me know I was not alone.

As the first squirrel approached me from behind, I turned around slowly and offered him a peanut. His dark, curious eyes followed my hand as it neared him. He reached out and grabbed the peanut from my fingers, eagerly cracking the shell, searching desperately for the treasure inside.

As the others descended from the trees, I sat on the ground, hoping that this would make me less intimidating to them. A second squirrel climbed up onto my knee and reached for the bag of peanuts hidden in my lap. Excitement overwhelmed me as I moved the bag out of his reach and instead handed him just one. A third squirrel jumped up onto my shoulder, patiently waiting for me to give him his piece.

After a few minutes I had about a dozen squirrels gathered all around and on top of me. I watched them happy and content, as they finished the last of their afternoon snacks. When they were done I turned the brown paper sack upside down with my left hand.

"Sorry guys. No more," I told them, extending the other empty hand so they could see that I was telling the truth.

I slowly began to get up so that my gentle movements would allow them plenty of time to jump down and be on their merry way. I tossed the empty sack into a nearby trash can and grabbed my duffle bag, slinging it over my shoulder as I turned and headed toward the beach. Feeling their eyes staring at me, I looked back and saw that the little fellows were now trying to follow me silently.

"Seriously guys. No more!"

Again, I held out my hands to show the squirrels that I had nothing more to offer them. They just sat up on their haunches, staring at me in wide-eyed bewilderment. I began to laugh at their puzzled expressions and the sound of that finally caused them to scatter.

When I reached the end of the trees, I climbed up to the top of the sand dune and stood there for a moment to take in the scenery. The sun, still high on the horizon, was shining in the distance, making the sugary white sand gleam. The beach was relatively empty so I would only have to share it with just a few other people.

The tranquility was one of the reasons that I'd grown to love this island. It emanated such an Old Florida vibe, which was what I imagined that it had been like before everyone decided to come to the sunshine state, overpopulating the beaches with tourists and overpriced hotels.

My only companions now were an old man, who stood at the end of a concrete pier fishing, and a young couple strolling hand in hand toward the northern part of the beach. Neither was paying me any attention and I felt as if I had the whole beach to myself.

The heat was unbearable without the shade of the trees in the park, so I threw my bag down on the sand, quickly yanked off my t-shirt and headed swiftly toward the cool, inviting ocean.

The blue-green water was calm and refreshing. As I stood and jumped the light waves, schools of fish came over tickling my legs and feet. I ducked under the surface and let myself float as the water embraced me.

After a few minutes of peaceful serenity, I felt thoroughly cool and rejuvenated so I decided to get out. I laid down my towel, took a seat on top of it and let myself air-dry in the summer breeze.

I sat with my arms propped behind me, watching the ocean and thinking about my strange first day of school and the tingly feeling that I felt around Kat, Liam and especially Kailani. I wondered what that had been about and pondered if they could feel it too? At times it seemed like maybe they could, but how do you ask someone something like that without sounding like a freak?

After analyzing every moment I spent near Kailani, I still couldn't figure out if she liked me or not. As I sat there, lost in thought, I saw a small crab dart across the sand.

I reached out and picked him up from behind with my thumb and forefinger so that he couldn't pinch me with his stubby claws. I looked at him inquisitively as he struggled against my grip, legs flailing desperately through the air.

All of a sudden I felt a wave of anger flood through me. How odd. Just a moment before, I had felt so peaceful and serene.

I thought about my reactions to the contact with the fish and then the squirrels. I started toying in my mind with a little theory, so I decided to test it out.

I sat the tiny crab down and immediately felt my temperament shift back to serene. I picked him back up, anger. Shocked that my mood had fluctuated just as I thought it would, I repeated this process again several times before coming to the shocking conclusion that my theory was correct. I was absorbing the emotions that were radiating from these animals.

Impossible!

I had a hard time believing it, but it seemed true. Whenever I touched them, I could somehow feel how they felt. It was like I had some kind of weird empathy or something.

I asked myself the question, why here? I had never been able to do this in Alaska. Why now?

Still slightly distracted by my recent discovery, I looked at the sky as some seagulls dipped into the water to catch some small fish for dinner. I grabbed the loaf of bread out of my bag and began breaking it into small pieces. I then stood up and threw a piece out as far as I could into the air, toward the water. The splat of the bread as it landed in the shallow water attracted the attention of one of the birds.

I threw another piece up. This time the gull flew down to catch it in mid-air.

After a few moments, a large group of them were standing on the sand or hovering right in front of me, waiting to catch the crumbs that I threw. As hard as I tried, I could not feel anything from these birds so I decided that there had to be physical contact in order for me to make the emotional connection.

After the bread ran out, I sat back down on my towel to watch the sun set. Once the seagulls realized that they weren't getting any more food, some went back to their previous dive bombing fishing tactics and others simply flew away.

I could see a couple of dolphins swimming in the distance, their dorsal fins occasionally popping up as they chased one another back and forth across the horizon. I sat there, completely motionless, taking in all of the beauty that surrounded me. I don't know how much time had passed. All I know is that I didn't even think about getting up until the sun had completely set.

The moon was bright in the sky, grinning like the Cheshire cat over the bay that was behind me. It's smile was comforting, almost like it was happy to see me, happy to see that I was happy. I couldn't help but to return the smile.

As I walked home on the beach, bathed in the moonlight, the waves splashed up and onto my ankles from time to time. The night was quiet and I was so absorbed in my thoughts, I passed the path that cut across the street to my home so I had to double back.

When I finally made it to the house, all of the lights were out, which let me know that Alana had not yet made it home. After turning the front porch light on for her, I made myself another sandwich before heading up to my room.

I sat on my bed fiddling with my guitar a bit before deciding to write a quick email to Abby and my dad, letting them both know I was doing okay. I briefly described my first day of school, making sure to exclude all of the weirdness. After I was finished, I found myself so bored that I decided just to go to bed early.

I burrowed into the cozy black comforter and grabbed the moonstone that I still wore around my neck. I began tracing the raised silver arrow with my finger absentmindedly as I looked up at my artificial sky trying to remember each of the constellations. I stared at them for so long and so hard that they eventually seemed to glow brighter until they became orbs of light that seemed to move and float through the air.

They started to spin and dance. No longer were they just above me. The blackness around them seemed to shrink to nothing as they floated closer. Suddenly I felt blinded by the abrupt onslaught of the blazing orbs. I felt myself sink deeper into the bed.

Next, as if a light switch had been flipped, my view went

abrubtly dark. I saw a faint blue light and the closer I got, the more I thought I recognized Kailani's image in the middle of it, even though the picture was murky and unclear. Her hair seemed to float weightlessly around her angelic face and her eyes were closed. She was smiling as if she were enjoying the images of a pleasant dream.

I drifted closer, unable to resist her luring beauty. With her eyes still closed, she shifted restlessly, whispering my name. Her smile then disappeared and her features contorted as she repeated my name again, but this time she sounded worried, as if her dream had quickly turned into a nightmare.

Everything then went dark again and I floated through the darkness, unable to tell which way was up or down. When the orbs of light reappeared around me I heard someone's voice this time. It was light and airy and sounded almost like wind chimes.

"Aden."

More voices chimed in, now with more urgency.

"Aden, come home!" they murmured.

The first voice was still the clearest though, as it said, "Come home, Aden. Beware. Danger!"

At the word danger, I startled awake. Realizing that it was just a dream I looked at the clock on the wall, it read three am. I got up to make sure that Alana had made it home safely. She lay in her bed, sound asleep, so I went down to the kitchen, grabbed a glass of water then headed back upstairs to try to get some more rest.

I looked up at the stars again and thought about the weird dream.

"Come home?" I was already home.

What was that all about?

I remembered the look on Kailani's face in my dream, when she had first smiled, then whispered my name. Maybe she does like me. Maybe this dream was meant to give me the courage to go and talk to her, ask her out.

Then I remembered what Michael had said. "Kaili doesn't date."

Maybe she just hadn't met the right person yet. Maybe by some chance she was holding out for a good guy, someone smart and sweet, someone who would love her like she was the only one who would ever have his heart.

That someone was me.

I would never know unless I took a chance and asked her, but what if she rejected me? I thought about this for a little while. I had promised myself and my father that I would be more open to love. I knew that I had to do this, more for myself than anything. Even if she did say no, at least I would know that I tried and wouldn't always have to wonder what if?

Before I fell back asleep, I decided that I was going to do it, ask her out. I thought about the Homecoming Dance that we would be planning together. I could see it all play out so perfectly in my head. Tomorrow, after school, I would throw all caution and insecurity to the wind. I would casually get Kailani's attention after World Lit then I would make some brilliant, funny comment and she would laugh.

Then I would bravely and unhesitatingly ask her to go with me to the dance, then, of course, she would have to say yes.

"Your majesty. I just wanted to give you a quick report on how your son is doing."

"Very well."

"After his first day of school today, I was watching him as he went to the beach." Faelyn swallowed hard.

"His powers are already beginning to show," she continued. *"I believe that he is beginning to realize that something strange is happening to him. He seemed even more fascinated with the animals than usual. He was talking to squirrels and playing with a crab, looking puzzled as he picked it up, then put it down, over and over again."*

Melissa thought about this for a moment.

"I didn't expect this to start happening so soon," she said.

"Neither did I."

"Stay close to him. Remember you must never reveal yourself until the time has come."

Faelyn nodded her understanding.

"As you wish, your majesty."

Chapter 6

Courage

So, I know I said tomorrow, but it's a lot easier to say that you're gonna do something while you're sitting in the comfort of your own room, without the worry of anyone judging you. You are able to build up a false confidence that quickly fades away in the light of the next day. So, actually it was a few days later before I even worked up the courage to talk to Kailani, much less ask her the question that I was hoping to get a yes to.

It was Friday afternoon and the whole school was abuzz with excitement for the first football game of the season. Even though tonight was an away game, it was all everyone was talking about. What made it even more exciting was that they would be playing our neighboring rivals, Bayside High. This morning the school had thrown a huge pep rally in the gym to get everyone pumped up and all the football players had worn their jerseys and the cheerleaders all had on their uniforms to promote school spirit. That meant today at lunch, Alana, Kailani and I were the only ones not dressed in the matching garb.

I watched the clock tick on the wall as I sat through World Literature, nervously waiting for the last bell to ring. Today after school we were scheduled to have our first Homecoming Committee meeting. They had even made an announcement on the intercom this morning, reminding all of the members and letting everyone else know that they still needed a few more volunteers.

I'd asked Alana if she wanted to come help, since she would have to wait on me anyway, but she gave me a scornful "No way!" and tossed me the keys to the Civic. She said she would just catch a ride home with Jason.

Glancing back up at the clock, I was now counting down. Two more minutes. I stared at the back of Kailani's head. Her long blond hair was pulled back into a low ponytail that was tied with a lavender ribbon, perfectly matching her cashmere cardigan. I took a few long, slow breaths, reminding myself that I could do this.

As soon as the bell rang, Mr. Mitchell, whose first name I had since learned was Ron, asked us to kindly make room for the other students who were slowly trickling in.

Kat was the last one to appear through the door. Her bright red uniform read MHS in blue letters across the vest and I noticed as she lithely strutted in, her skirt flashed small triangles of the same shade of vivid blue as the initials. Her dark blond hair was twisted up in the front, with the back carefully done in tons of meticulous curls, and behind her left ear she had tucked two feathers that dangled, one red and one blue, to match her uniform. You couldn't help but notice the excessive amount of glitter that she wore. The florescent lights were bouncing off of it, making every inch of her exposed skin sparkle. She walked by Kailani, then me and settled down into a seat near the back of the room.

Once everyone had been seated, the meeting was then called to order.

"First order of business. We will need someone to volunteer as the president of the committee," Ron declared.

Brooke was the only one to raise her hand, so she was just as quickly nominated for the role.

"Next, we need to decide upon an overall theme. I would like each person who has a suggestion to come up to the front of the room and present their idea."

Brooke raised her hand again and Mr. Mitchell motioned for her to take the floor.

Confidently, she presented her idea as if it had already been discussed, voted and agreed upon by all.

"I was thinking we could do a Fall festival theme, with lots of rich burgundy and gold decor. We could even get a bunch of multicolored leaves to scatter around the dance floor and some cornucopias to decorate the refreshment tables."

Another girl, who I still had not yet met, suggested that we make it a costume party or a masquerade ball, since the dance fell on the day before Halloween. That to me sounded like a lot more fun.

Kat was last and provided the only other suggestion.

"How about, since we live in Florida and rarely see the cold weather, we do an ice castle theme and decorate in all white and silver. We can even have ice sculptures and a fake snow machine."

I looked around the room and saw everyone's head was nodding, charmed by the lovely tone of her voice and how appealing she made her idea seem. The only one who, ever so slightly, still looked apprehensive was Brooke. As Kat walked by her desk, on the way back to her seat, I saw her gently touch Brooke on the arm then bend over to whisper something into her ear.

Mr. Mitchell then asked everyone to vote by a show

of hands on which theme they would like the most. The Halloween and Fall festival ideas seemed to now be suddenly forgotten, even by their own presenters.

Everyone had voted with Kat on her ice castle theme, even Brooke. I looked back and saw a smug, satisfactory smile plastered on Kat's face. Once she realized that I was looking in her direction, her expression quickly morphed to chagrin, then sheepishness, as her eyes lowered when she looked away. When she glanced back at me a few seconds later, I could see the confusion that was clouding her face.

After several more questions on the food, music and other details, Ron adjourned the meeting. He asked Brooke to stay behind with him for a few more minutes more to help with a little more of the detailed planning.

I steeled myself. This was my chance! Kat quickly said goodbye to her sister then hurried out the door to catch the bus waiting to carry all of the cheerleaders over to Bayside.

As we walked toward the door, Kailani was only a few steps ahead of me.

"Hey, Kaili! Wait up!" I said.

She turned to look at me with a polite smile radiating her stunning features.

"Oh, Hi Aden. How was your first week of school?" she asked casually.

"It was all right. Not half as bad as I thought it would be."

Her smile turned apologetic as we exited the classroom before heading toward the parking lot.

I took a deep breath, forcing myself to continue.

"I've been meaning to tell you, since the first day I saw you, how much I loved your singing."

Stopping in her tracks, she turned to me with wide eyes. "You can remember that?"

Unsure of quite how to respond, I said "Of course I can remember that. It was only a few days ago."

She nodded slightly then kept walking beside me, looking forward at the ground. I noticed the closer we got to the parking lot, the lighter her sun kissed skin was becoming.

After walking in silence for the few seconds that seemed to stretch on forever, she stopped again, turning to look me straight in the eye.

"You can't remember my singing now, can you?"

My eyes squinted in confusion and I laughed a little, nervously. Was she serious?

"Of course I can. You have the most beautiful voice that I've ever heard. It is not so easily forgotten."

Her inquisitive eyes looked back at mine. Her gaze was intense and it seemed as if she were searching for something there. She then blinked, as if she had just realized how crazy she must have just seemed.

"Right. I mean, thank you," she said, turning quickly to start walking again.

The intense heat from the sun doubled when we hit the black asphalt and by the time we arrived at her Jeep, I was beginning to sweat. I could feel the droplets trickling down the back of my neck. I looked over at Kailani. Her white skin was pore-less and perfect, without the slightest hint of perspiration. She gave me her perfectly polite, but dazzling smile.

"Well, thanks for walking me to my car," she said.

This was it. If I didn't do it now, I would lose my chance, maybe for good.

"Actually, there was something that I wanted to ask you."

I paused for a second, trying to read her expression.

"I was just wondering," I said, "I know it's a little early, but I was thinking that since we would be planning the dance together, maybe you might want to go with me?"

Her face lit up, but only for a split second. Then her expression rapidly changed to regret and I knew what her answer was going to be before she said it aloud.

"Oh, well I would love to, but unfortunately Michael asked me the other day and I already said yes."

Michael? Of course, I realized. That's why he told me Kaili doesn't date. Obviously she does. He was just trying to eliminate the competition so that he would stand a better chance when he tried to talk to her himself.

I tried to hide the anger I could feel welling up inside of me.

"Well, that's okay. Maybe we could just hang out sometime, you know, go have dinner or something."

"I'm not so sure that would be such a good idea," she said, "I don't want you to get the wrong impression. Maybe we could just be friends?"

"Of course. Yeah. Friends. We can just be friends. That's what I meant."

The anger and embarrassment were making the inflections in my voice sound awkward and I realized my head was bobbing up and down as I spoke, like some stupid dashboard bobble head.

"Okay, great. I'll see you around then?" I managed to say.

"See you around,"

After a little wave, I turned and started walking briskly to my car, fighting the urge to run. I couldn't seem to get there fast enough.

Well, that didn't go quite like I planned, I thought to myself. I can't believe Michael! That sneaky little snake!

I was so lost in my own private and frustrated thoughts that I didn't even see Brooke running up until she was right there beside me.

"Hey, Aden!"

"Oh. Hi Brooke. How's it going?"

"Great! Ron had a few more really good ideas to surprise everyone, but he also had some not so good ones too." She rolled her eyes. "It's a lot to deal with, but I'm glad that I'm there to help with making all of the decisions."

Suddenly, I remembered the meeting, that moment with Kat. Something strange had happened and it was really bugging me. I decided to ask Brooke about it to try to figure it out.

"How come you gave up on your idea for the theme so quickly?"

"What idea?"

"You know, the Fall festival theme with all the burgundy and gold decorations."

She looked at me with a blank expression on her face, then shook her head, as if waking from a dream.

"I don't know. I guess I just forgot about that. Kat's idea just sounded so much more appealing once I really thought about it, plus, I have this brand new, white Calvin Klein dress that I've just been dying to wear."

As she mentioned her dress, her features became much more animated.

"Right," I said.

"Listen, I was thinking," Brooke said suddenly, "if you don't already have a date for the dance, maybe you would like to take me?"

I watched her nervously tuck her short blond hair behind her ear and stare at me with her anxious, bright green eyes. I thought about how bad it felt to be rejected myself so recently and couldn't bear to inflict that same pain on someone else, even if they weren't exactly my favorite person in the world. Besides, I hadn't wanted to go with anyone except Kailani. Since I knew now that wasn't happening, why not just make Brooke happy?

"Sure," I said, trying not to sound too defeated.

"Great! It will be so much fun! I'm gonna throw a huge party at my parents beach house afterwards, so you will have to come to that too! Alana said Jason is taking her, so maybe we could double date?! I'll talk to you more about it later. Right now I've got to run."

"Alright," I said. I barely got the word out before she turned, smoothing down her uniform, then bolting for the nearby bus that was still patiently waiting on its last cheerleader.

Yeah. Great! Spending the whole evening with Brooke and Jason. Already I was beginning to regret my decision.

Vanessa clenched her fist. It had been far too long since she had lost track of this boy and Nitra had still been unsuccessful in her attempt to track him down.

Sitting back on her throne made of human bones, Vanessa's mind went back to the day that Maggie had told her about the prophecy.

She'd told Vanessa that this boy was the only one who could unite the stones, the magical stones that harnessed the powers of the gods. These stones were essential to Vanessa's plan. She knew the whereabouts of most of them, but she needed to make sure that she had all of them if this was going to work.

Vanessa remembered the last part of the prophecy and thought about the other individual who it had named. A startling thought then came to mind.

Perhaps they had been looking in the wrong spot. Perhaps it was time that she paid closer attention to what her older sister had been up to.

Chapter 7
Snow Globe

After many weeks of preparation, the day of the Homecoming dance had finally arrived. I checked the forecast earlier this morning and it said that we would have clear, sunny skies for the duration of the day, with a low of 68 degrees tonight. Here in Florida the Fall is only slightly cooler than the Summer.

Alana and Brooke had planned everything out for us. They even set it all up so that we would have plenty of time to go and have dinner together before the dance. All afternoon long they had been out and about getting their hair, make-up and nails done.

Three times already this past week, Brooke made a point to let me know that her parents had left town. They'd decided to fly to Aspen to spend a month skiing at one of their resorts. Apparently they owned a lot of them. This meant that there would be no parental supervision at her party. Her parents, the Kinsingtons, had made arrangements for William, the chauffeur, to pick us up in the private limo and had instructed him to drive us around for the entire evening, bringing us safely back to their home later tonight.

The limo pulled into our driveway at five o'clock sharp. I had wanted to wear just my undershirt and pants for the more casual look, but Alana insisted that I add the jacket and the tie to make our group photos more formal.

Alana walked into my room just as I was standing in front

of the mirror, fussing with my long silver tie. I felt like it was choking me. Underneath it, I could feel my mother's necklace, which I wore all the time, pressing into my skin.

"The limo's here," Alana told me.

"I know. I'm ready," I said, still fiddling with the tie.

I looked over at her. She was wearing a long, emerald green dress that complimented her eyes. It contrasted nicely with her curly, red updo, making it seem much more vibrant.

"Well, don't you clean up nicely," I teased.

"Oh, shut up Aden." She rolled her eyes, but her face blushed, betraying her pretend irritation at my comment.

"I'm just giving you a hard time. I think you really do look pretty tonight, cuz."

"Thank you."

She stood there for a moment, watching me as I continued to struggle with my tie.

"Do you need any help with that?" she asked as she walked over to stand in front of me.

I dropped my hands in wordless acceptance and just stood there, letting her fix me up.

It wasn't long before we heard the doorbell ring.

"Are you ready?" I asked Alana.

She gave me her most enthusiastic grin and nodded. I then held out my arm to her, helping her down the stairs as we both walked down to meet my date at the door.

Brooke was standing there in a model's pose, wearing a knee-length white satin dress that reminded me more of lingerie than formal wear. Her dangling earrings were encrusted in diamonds that matched her silver, bejeweled heels, which had to be at least six inches high.

"Wow!" was the only word that came out of my mouth.

"I know, right! I'm hot!" she said as she ran her hands down her body, proudly presenting her curves.

She then grabbed mine and Alana's arm, pulling us toward the limo. She talked cheerfully and non-stop all the way to Bradenton.

"Did I already tell you guys that my parents will be out of town tonight?" she asked.

"Yes!" Alana and I replied in perfect unison.

Once at Jason's house, we let his mom take a few pictures before heading back to Anna Maria Island for dinner at Beach House. The restaurant's outdoor patio was separated from the beach by a small rock wall that you could look over to watch the sunset as you ate. Unfortunately, tonight we had to sit inside because the entire patio had been reserved for a wedding reception. I was thankful that the hostess had at least given us a window seat. That way I was able to pass the time by people watching when I got bored with the conversation at our table.

When the newly wed couple got up to dance together for the first time, I watched the way they gazed into each other's eyes as they twirled blissfully around the dance floor. It was obvious that they could hear the music, because their moves were timed perfectly, but it seemed as if to them everything and everyone else had ceased to exist. Their eyes never left each other except for the brief moment when the bride rested her cheek contently on her new husband's chest. Happiness radiated from the young couple and I couldn't help but hope that one day I would be that happy too.

In that fleeting moment of hope, Kailani's face flickered

into my mind and I thought about the fact that in an hour or two I would be watching the girl of my dreams dance like that with Michael. Suddenly I lost my appetite.

Kailani had said that we could be friends and surprisingly, now we really were. She had been over to my house several times to help me study for upcoming tests and I was amazed to learn how smart she was. Her intelligence only served to strengthen my attraction to her. I had even gone to the Homecoming game last week with her to watch as her sister and Liam got crowned the King and Queen of the Homecoming court during half time.

Now here we were, stuck in the friend zone, which wasn't exactly what I was hoping for. Even with this progress she still seemed to be keeping me at a distance for some reason. I could recognize the signs. After all, it was something I had become quite an expert at.

After dinner, I had to pick up the check for everyone, since Jason conveniently left his wallet at home. We then rode to the high school gym where the dance was being held.

Luckily, I had been on the food committee, which mainly consisted of picking out the hors d'ouerves that would be served, then mailing the menu to the caterers. The decoration committee, to which Kailani was assigned, had been required to stay after school this entire week, even late last night after the Homecoming game, to finish with the last minute decor.

When we walked through the double doors, I was amazed at how much they had accomplished. The ceiling was covered in white balloons with silver metallic ribbons hanging down in spirals throughout the air. Faux Birch trees covered the walls with bare branches that glowed from the blue up-lighting, giving an aesthetic winter wonderland ambiance to the gym. Artificial snow was pushed into drifts around the corners of the room and the dance floor.

The booth where the DJ was playing looked like it was made from stacked blocks of ice, and elaborate ice sculptures stood as centerpieces throughout the room, each on a pristine white table cloth. There was even blue punch that ran through a waterfall made of ice. It was designed to chill the beverage, as it pooled into the bottom reservoir.

We were only running a little bit late, but the dance floor was already crowded with lots of couples, including Kat and Liam, who were dancing gracefully near the center. Kat's dress was a short and colored hot pink-coral, with sheer fabric that hung in several longer intervals past the bottom hem. The top was covered in rhinestones that gradually became more and more sparse the further down the dress you looked.

As she twisted and twirled, the sheer fabric floated up around her, reminding me of a beautifully glimmering jellyfish whose tentacles were lifted by a gentle ocean current. Her hair was done in loose curls threaded with a golden tinsel that twinkled in the lights. Gold shoes completed the ensemble and her graceful dance moves put everyone else that was surrounding her to shame.

I looked around the room, knowing Kailani had to be somewhere near. I could feel her presence.

She had told me yesterday that she and her sister would be riding to the dance together with their dates and I spotted her over at the picture backdrop that had the same decorative birch trees around it. They were placed into an archway so that the photographer could center each couple underneath.

A second later Kailani looked my way, as if she could feel that I was looking at her.

The blue lighting only intensified the blue of her sparkling eyes, leaving almost no trace of any green tint. She flashed me an exuberant smile and waved in my direction. She was so stunningly gorgeous, in such an effortless way, that I had to force my hand up to return the wave.

Her golden hair was pinned up elegantly with a few wispy tendrils that were framing her beautiful face. Her ice blue dress was woven with a subtle silver shimmer, and delicate diamond straps held it up on her slender shoulders. She turned toward Michael as the photographer snapped their picture and I could see that the back was cut low, all the way down to her waist. There was also a slit on one side that went up to the middle of her thigh.

As I stood there staring, I hardly even realized that Brooke had run off to go compare dresses with some of her girlfriends.

I felt Alana touch me on the arm.

"Hey, Aden. Jason and I are gonna go dance, if you need us."

"Okay. Have fun. Behave!" I said with a smirk.

She giggled a little before replying, "And what kind of fun do you think that would be?"

I looked back at Kailani and saw Michael walk away, heading in the direction of the refreshment table. I decided to go over to her and say hi.

"Enchanté, mademoiselle," I exclaimed as I grabbed her hand then kissed it.

Those were the only two words I knew in French and I'd always wanted to use them. Immediately, it felt too cheesy and I decided to add something else a little more true to how I really felt.

"You look unbelievable."

"Thank you," she answered with a smile. "You look pretty unbelievable yourself."

"I can't believe how good the gym looks," I told her, looking around. "You guys did a fantastic job with all the decorations."

"Yeah, well it better! We were here til almost midnight last night. I'm glad that you like them. I tried really hard to make my sister's vision become a reality."

"Wasn't she here to help?"

"No. She tried to get in the gym last night, but I wouldn't let her. I wanted it to be a surprise!"

"Well, that was very altruistic of you. I just saw her on the dance floor and it looks like she's having a wonderful time."

"I think so too! A Ball fit for a Queen!" She giggled at her own little joke.

It was just like Kailani to stay behind the scenes, giving her sister the spotlight that she craved, letting her shine, when in my eyes it was Kailani who was truly the star.

Her silky voice interrupted my thoughts.

"Hey! You and I should take a picture while we're here."

She grabbed me around the waist with one arm and pulled me closer to her. I placed my arm gently around her shoulders, hoping that she couldn't feel just how fast my heart was beating. On the count of three I couldn't help but smile.

After the impromptu picture was taken, out of the corner of my eye I saw Michael returning with their drinks. Not trusting myself to be civil with him, I quickly excused myself.

"Well, I better go find my date," I told Kaili rather reluctantly, then added, "Save me a dance for later?"

"Of course, I will."

I then started wondering if maybe, just maybe, we could be more than just friends, but as soon as I turned away from Kailani, I saw Brooke walking toward me.

"Hey! I've been looking for you. Let's go dance."

We made our way out to the crowded dance floor that consisted of a big white fabric sheet they had pulled tight to cover the gymnasium floor. On top of it was fake snow that had been infused with glitter which sparkled softly in the pale blue lighting.

I wasn't the best dancer, but I had a little rhythm, thanks to my best friend Abby. Back in middle school, she had spent several hours with me up in her room, teaching me a few moves so that I wouldn't feel like a complete idiot when it came to school dances.

Brooke and I were surrounded by alot of couples and several all girl groups dancing, while laughing, as the music played. I glanced around and spotted Alana and Jason over near the back of the gym. They were dancing where it was a little more private.

When the song changed to something a little slower, all of the girl groups left, leaving just the couples on the dance floor.

"This is fun, right?" Brooke asked, pulling me closer.

"Yeah, sure is," I said looking over her shoulder. I saw Kailani and Michael were coming over onto the dance floor not too far from us.

Kailani's eyes met mine and she smiled at me over Michael's shoulder. As they slowly spun around, I was left looking at the revealing back of her dress, watching it hug all her flawless curves in just the right places. I looked up and saw that Michael was grinning at me as he took his hand, moving it to her lower back.

Ugh, I couldn't stand him.

He was gloating! What I really wanted to do right now was just go over there and knock that smug little grin off his repulsive face.

Every time Kailani would turn my way, she would peek at me over Michael's shoulder. I didn't get it. Why were girls so confusing? Her actions were telling me that she liked me, but she had made it clear that she didn't want to be with me, she just wanted to be friends.

We played our little game of peek-a-boo for quite a while, and every time that Michael turned to face me again, I forced myself to look away.

When I glanced over at Alana and Jason, I noticed right away that something was definitely wrong. They were no longer smiling or dancing and Jason looked really angry.

As I continued to watch, Alana backed away from him as he took a step toward her, grabbing her arm so hard that she winced from the pain while trying hard at the same time not to attract anyone's attention.

Immediately, I excused myself from Brooke and rushed over to see what was going on. I tapped Jason on the shoulder.

"Hey, man! What's your problem?" I asked angrily.

"That's none of your business!" he told me. "This is between me and..."

He never got out the last word because I punched him right in the mouth.

I'd hit him so hard that he instantly fell down to the dance floor. At that moment, I silently thanked my dad for teaching me how to throw a good punch. I'd never been much of a fighter, but my dad had insisted that I know how to defend myself at least.

I heard the people gathering all around us to watch our fight. My temper had gotten the best of me and I realized I could barely even hear Alana as she screamed at us to stop fighting. Jason had gotten back on his feet again and tried to tackle me around the waist. I used his own momentum against him and stepped out of the way just in time before slamming him back down to the floor.

"Don't you ever touch my cousin like that again!" I shouted, punching him once more as he lay on the floor.

The next thing I know, I was getting pulled back by several of his team members. Some of them were holding me, while others started kicking me, throwing punches into my ribs and back. While his teammates still held me, Jason got up and punched me hard, in the stomach.

"Cheap shot," I muttered, as soon as I recovered my breath.

Suddenly, the double doors of the gym blew wide open with a violent gust of wind. Debris blew through the air and swirled around the room as particles of synthetic snow were lifted up into a whirlwind blizzard. No one could see for several seconds and the students around me began to panic and scream. It was like being trapped in the middle of a giant snow globe with no way out.

Then, just as suddenly as it had started, the winds subsided and were gone.

I felt the guys release me and I looked over to see Kailani staring at me. Her eyes were wide with snow particles clinging to her hair.

"Go! Now!" she mouthed at me.

Confused, I only stared back at her.

A moment later the music teacher, Mr. Spencer, ran up to me in his tacky brown fedora. He, like everyone else, was covered in the glittery, white polymer.

"Aden! Jason! You're both out of here! As well as any of you other guys who participated in this little brawl!"

The other team members looked around at each other. None of them wanted to take any of the blame.

Mrs. Hall, my P. E. teacher, suddenly appeared and spoke to us all.

"I'm sorry, you guys, but the rules are the rules. No fighting." Her tone was soft and apologetic, yet firm at the same. "Both of you will show up at the principal's office first thing Monday morning to receive your punishment."

I looked through the crowd for Alana and spotted Brooke with her arm around my cousin's shoulders, leading her out the back door. Brooke turned her head to look back at me, to make sure that I was coming.

Turning back to Jason I told him forcefully, "I don't care how you get home, but you're not riding with us."

I walked away, then yelled back to him, "And you better not show up at Brooke's party either."

The music began to play again and Mr. Spencer and Mrs. Hall busied themselves with ushering the students away, telling them to go back to their previous activities.

I looked over at Kailani one last time, suddenly sorry that I had to leave, disappointed because now we wouldn't be able to have our dance together.

"I'm so sorry." I mouthed the words to her from across the room then turned to make my exit.

Chapter 8

After-Party

We pulled up to the wrought iron gates in front of Brooke's home, on the northern side of Anna Maria Island. Her house was enormous, even bigger than my aunt's, yet done in the same Mediterranean style architecture.

When we walked through the heavy, rustic double doors at the entrance, I saw the inside of the mansion was elaborately decorated with large, winding staircases, robust statues and marble floors. Just inside the main entrance we passed the refreshment tables, where I saw a butler, dressed in the traditional black and white tuxedo, setting out the food and drinks. Clearly caught off guard that we had arrived so much earlier than expected, he quickly recovered, apologized to Brooke for the setup not being already complete, then hastened to finish up.

Of course, we were only the first to arrive. Even after dropping Alana off at home, we still managed to get here before anyone else. I still felt bad about leaving Alana there all by herself, even though she had yelled at me the entire way home for embarrassing her in front of all of her friends. I'd asked if she wanted me to stay with her to keep her company. I practically begged her to say yes, but she was too mad and unfortunately insisted that I go with Brooke to the party and "leave her the hell alone."

Brooke led me to the back of the house, through a floor-to-ceiling sliding glass door that led out to the pool area. A DJ was already out here setting up in the corner to our left. He was wearing a large pair of lime green headphones, listening to his tracks and adjusting the music. Unlike the butler, he seemed impervious to our arrival. His shift had not yet begun so I figured he must have already been paid in advance because of his lack of interest in anything outside of his own little world.

I noticed a keg in the middle of one of the tables set up in the opposite corner. Surrounding it was a mountain of red solo cups. A bartender stood at attention at another table, right beside the big red mountain. He was ready to mix all types of cocktails upon request. In front of him there were stacks of five different types of glasses. Behind him, there were four shelves that had been stocked with twenty different kinds of premium liquor, wine and flavored liqueurs.

"Would you like a beer?" Brooke asked me.

"No thanks. I don't really drink."

"Suit yourself," she replied as she grabbed one of the red plastic cups and started to fill it up.

I was surprised, not at the fact that she was drinking, but because she had poured the beer herself, without asking any of the help to do it for her.

I saw a group of guys on the stage that was located at the far end of the pool. They were setting up, fine tuning their instruments, getting them ready to play them later.

"Who are they?" I asked Brooke, pointing to the stage.

"Oh. That's We the Kings. They're a local band from Bradenton that made it big. They've been friends with our family for years! I called them a few days ago and convinced them to come tonight to play a few of their most popular songs."

As she spoke, I noticed a few of the other students from our school were just beginning to arrive. I guessed the little interruption at the gym had been the perfect excuse for some of them to go ahead and leave early. When I thought about just how hard Kalaini had worked on the gym, I felt sick.

I recognized one of the blond boys from our Physics class coming out through the back door, walking in my direction.

When he finally reached me, he asked, "Is Alana Okay?"

"She's fine. She's just at home, said she just didn't really feel like partying anymore, you know."

"Yeah, of course," he said, looking rather disappointed. "I was just hoping that she would be here, that's all. Will you tell her I said hi?"

"Sure thing."

I watched as he turned, then made his way over to the nearby refreshments.

I sat down on one of the oversized lounge chairs and propped my feet up, already over this. More people trickled in, including many of the guys from the football team, who stopped by my chair to apologize. Most of their apologies were short and sweet, but a few of them were a little longer.

Most of them said that they hadn't seen what happened before. They only saw me once I was standing over Jason so they came to help their team mate. After the story had gotten around that he had actually deserved it, they realized that they had made a mistake and told me they were sorry for jumping to conclusions.

As I continued to lounge on the outdoor chaise, watching the people arrive, I realized that the dance must have ended. Within a span of what seemed like five blinks, the entire pool area was packed. As if triggered by some silent cue, the band began to play and everyone swarmed to the stage.

I tried now to get out of the middle of the large crowd so I pushed my way toward the house. As I was almost to the back door, I felt the cool tingles igniting throughout my body again and looked up to see that Kailani had arrived with Kat, Liam and Michael. She didn't walk toward me with the others, instead I saw her head straight for the beach. Instinctually I followed her direction.

Brooke grabbed my arm as she saw me emerging from the crowd. Preoccupied, I hadn't seen her, yet she had been standing right there in front of me. Already intoxicated, she must have thought that I had been looking for her because she then pulled me back toward her house.

"Do you want to go somewhere quieter? I could show you my room."

"Maybe later," I said, still looking toward the beach.

"We can hook up if you want," she said as she ran a finger down my chest and gave me her best sexy pout, as if silently pleading for me to say yes. She continued to look at me as she batted her eyelashes, but I could see that her head was weaving a little from the beer.

Oh boy, I thought to myself. I knew I now had to quickly come up with an excuse for saying no, while at the same time trying my best not to hurt her feelings.

"Well, actually, I was just going to go grab us a drink. You go ahead and go up and I'll meet you there in a few."

This satisfied her and she turned back toward the door so I took off in the opposite direction. I made it past the pool and to the refreshment table before I glanced back, just in time to see her go into the house, then head back toward the stairs.

I knew I had to hurry up and get out of here before she remembered that I had no idea where her room was. I was hoping that she would get all the way up to the second floor then go pass out before she realized that anything was amiss.

Elated my plan had worked, I turned back around, headed toward the beach and almost ran smack into Michael. He was standing there with a beer in his hand.

"Whoa! Hey, man!" he said to me, "Have you seen Brooke?"

"Actually she's in her room. She said she wasn't feeling so good so she went to go lie down for a while."

Call it what you want. It wasn't technically a lie. She certainly wasn't a hundo p and she did make a vague reference to lying down. I called it "being creative."

"Do you think that I should go up there and check on her?" Michael asked me.

"I would wait for a few minutes, but I think that would be a great idea," I said as enthusiastically as I could manage before taking the opportunity to then slip away before he had a chance to ask me any more questions.

Once I was able to break away from the party and was on the other side of the fence, I slung the formal jacket that I had been carrying over my right shoulder. I'd forgotten to leave it at home and had been afraid to set it down, worried that I might lose it.

I walked down a short pebble path, then stepped up onto a boardwalk that led to the dock, where the Kinsingtons housed their yacht. Before I realized that there were stairs coming off the side of it, I'd already jumped down to the sandy beach, placing my hand on one of their jet skis to use it for support.

The moon was full and bright tonight, giving the beach plenty of natural light and making it easy for me to spot Kailani sitting there beside the grasses on the dunes. It wasn't like I needed the light to find her. I could feel her energy pulling me to her. Silently, she was sitting there, cross-legged in the sand, drinking from her water bottle. She had already changed out of her formal dress and was now wearing a simple, light-green tank top with a pair of jeans. I still thought she looked just as beautiful as she had before.

As I approached, she looked at me with those big, bright eyes of hers, full of worry.

"Are you okay?" she asked me.

"I'm fine," I said, sitting down beside her.

"And Alana?"

"She's all right. A little shook up, but she'll be okay."

"I was so worried! Especially when I saw them all ganging up on you. I was just afraid that things were about to escalate out of control and you were about to be seriously injured."

"Oh, that was nothing," I told her, trying to laugh it off and pretend that I wasn't still sore, but when I looked up I could see her troubled face, with her golden skin, paled by the bright moonlight. Nothing in her expression told me that she was in the mood for any joking around.

"Thank you for worrying about me," I said, trying to reassure her. "Thankfully, there was that little blizzard that distracted everyone. That was pretty weird, huh?"

I eyed her suspiciously, before seeing her swallow thoughtfully.

"Yeah, weird," was all she said. She looked out at the ocean, I assumed to avoid making eye contact with me.

After a few moments I followed her gaze and joined her to

watch the full moon reflecting majestically off the waves. As we sat there in silence, listening to the sounds of the waves breaking on the sand, we could also faintly hear the music that the band was playing back at the party. To me it seemed as if they were playing just for us. When Kailani turned back to look at me, I continued to stare forward, but I could feel her inquisitive gaze.

"Aden?" she asked tentatively, "I know that you told me you used to live in Alaska with your father, but what about your mother? You never mentioned her. Where is she?"

"I have no idea," I told her as I slowly looked over into her eyes. "She left me with my dad when I was only a baby and never came back."

"Oh! I'm so sorry."

"Don't be. You can't really miss someone whom you've never even known." I said, placing my fingers gently on the necklace that was hidden beneath my shirt.

"I guess you're right," she said quietly.

I had the feeling that I was treading on thin ice, but I decided to go ahead and ask my question anyway.

"What about you? I know that you live with your grandmother, but what about your parents?"

"Well, I never knew either one of them. My father died tragically in some sort of accident before I was born and my mother passed while giving birth to my sister and me. The only parental figure I've ever known is my grandmother, Annessa."

She looked away, back out at the ocean.

"I'm sorry, too, then."

I reached over to touch her arm. Her skin was slightly

chilled, like the gulf night air. I was trying to be sympathetic, but I was suddenly distracted by how intense the tingling sensation became with physical touch of our skin. She looked over at me and I could tell that she could feel it too. She moved closer to me and I put my arm around her.

"You're so warm," she whispered as she laid her head on my shoulder.

We sat there in silence for a few more minutes. I was becoming almost hypnotized by the combination of the sound of the waves breaking on the shore and the constant current I felt thrumming through my body. I was hoping that she couldn't feel just how fast my heart was beating.

After a little while she turned to face my chest.

"I like your necklace," she said.

I looked down and saw that it must have somehow slipped out from under my shirt. It was glowing brightly, just like it had that night when my father had first given it to me.

"Thanks. It was a gift from my mother. It's the only thing I have of hers."

I looked down into Kailani's eyes and it was all I could do not to lean forward and kiss her. My attraction to her was magnetic and I didn't think I could stop it, even if I wanted to.

Imagine my surprise when she placed her cool fingers on my warm cheek and pulled me down to her as she pressed her lips to mine. I felt numb as the icy tingling intensified before slowly becoming hot.

Suddenly, she pulled away.

"I'm sorry," she whispered breathlessly.

The moment had empowered me to be bold.

"Well, I'm not." I said, taking a deep breath as I ran the

fingers of both hands through the soft golden hair that framed her face, pulling her back to me as I kissed her again.

This kiss was much more passionate and the heat it brought between us was undeniable. It felt like the earth beneath us was moving. I had never felt so alive before. My feelings of anxiety disappeared and excitement coursed through my veins, confusing me with all of the other new emotions that I could now feel flooding through me.

As I set one hand back down on the sand to steady myself, I realized that the earth really was moving. At least all the little sand granules around me were.

Hesitantly, I pulled away from Kailani, but she then moved toward me, reluctant for our kiss to end.

I looked down at my hand to see what was causing all of the movement beneath it and her gaze followed mine. Several baby sea turtles were digging their way up and out of the sand. I heard Kailani begin to laugh.

"They're hatchlings, baby Loggerheads."

We sat there for a while and watched them, laughing at how clumsily, yet eagerly they moved.

"Do you think that we should help them?" I asked her.

Shaking her head, she replied, "They know their way back to the sea. Even though they cannot see very well, they're instinctively attracted to the brightest light, which is usually the moon reflecting off the ocean. They have a good sense of direction. Even later, when they grow up, they will return to this very same beach, to lay their own eggs."

I stared at her while she spoke. Her eyes were pensive and it was like the story she told had taken her a million miles away.

Her eyebrows then pulled together, as if she'd become confused and she laughed before making the comment, "However, they really do seem to like you."

I looked down to see several of the baby turtles trying desperately to climb up my hand and onto my lap. Kailani was giggling.

"Well, I guess we could help them out," she said. "You know, make their journey a little bit faster."

We each scooped up a handful of the baby hatchlings and took them down to the shoreline. Gently we placed them onto the wet sand, right before a large wave came, sweeping them out to sea. After several trips back and forth, we released the last of the baby turtles. Kailani looked over at me and smiled.

"I think that we have now done our good deed for the day."

"Now, where were we?" I asked, grabbing her waist, playfully pulling her back toward me. I noticed that her skin was still cool to the touch as I stroked the back of my fingers down her arm.

"I can go get you my jacket if you'd like," I told her. "I left it just up there on the dunes."

"Oh, that's all right. I'm not cold."

I studied her face to see if she was telling me the truth or if she was just saying that so I wouldn't go through the trouble. I decided it didn't matter either way. I just used it as an excuse to wrap my arms around her instead.

"So," I said, kissing her forehead, "My aunt is having some kind of dinner party tomorrow night for Halloween and she said that I could bring someone if I wanted."

My kisses trailed down from her lips to her long, graceful neck as I said this, breaking up my words. Kailani pulled away, looking intently up at me as she began to smile, her eyes twinkling with mirth.

"Are you asking me to come and meet your family? Don't you think that it's a little too soon? I mean we've only just now had our very first kiss," she said with a southern accent, one side of her mouth twitching up.

"Well I..."

"I'm totally kidding! Of course, I'll come." She laughed for a second, but then her expression became earnest.

"There is something that I would like to tell you first though, before things between us get too serious." She hesitated. "The reason I haven't wanted to start anything with you isn't because I don't like you. I do, very much. Seeing you in danger tonight made me realize just how much I really do care about you. It's just that...I'm moving...in March."

"Moving? Where?"

"Denmark. Where my grandmother is originally from."

"What about Kat and Liam?"

"Kat will be coming with me in the Spring. Liam is coming with us too, but he will be leaving a little earlier, in a few days actually. He'll be going ahead with my grandmother to help her look for a place for us to live."

This explained Kailani's reservations about me. As much as I was sad to hear this news, I was also kind of relieved to know that the reason for her strange behavior wasn't because she didn't like me. She said she liked me a lot! I was doing the happy dance on the inside, but still trying to look calm and collected on the outside.

"But, you will be eighteen in March. Can't you just decide then to stay here if you want to?"

"It's not really an option for me. I have to go!"

I stared into her big blue eyes. They were locked onto mine, silently pleading me to leave it at that.

"Well, then I guess we'll just have to make the most of our last few months together," I said with a sigh, as I picked her up and twirled her around, trying to lighten the mood.

As I leaned down to kiss her again, a low rumble thundered in the distance and a flash of lightning lit up the sky, signaling the approach of a storm. Her eyes flickered from mine up to the sky, then back again.

"Time to go." she said.

"I was planning on leaving the party early anyway," I replied, thankful for the perfect excuse.

I released my arms from around her and took her hand, gently squeezing her cool fingers with mine as we walked back to the dunes to gather our things.

"Let's walk home," She said grinning, surprising me with her unexpected request. "It's not that far. I think that we'll have time."

She glanced toward the direction that the rumbling seemed to be coming from, then pulled me with both hands back toward the beach.

"Don't you need to tell your sister that you're leaving?" I asked.

"I already did," She replied with a sly grin, her turquoise eyes sparkling mischievously.

"There you are."

Vanessa grinned as she watched the same scene that her sister Annessa had just witnessed. Now she knew exactly where he was.

Full of disgust, she knew by the looks of things that she must act quickly. She was running out of time.

She summoned her daughter, who had recently returned home, into the room and greeted her enthusiastically at the door. Vanessa gripped Nitra's shoulder tightly as she told her the exciting news.

"It's time to go. Take Thad with you. He will help protect you in case there are any surprises."

Nitra raised her hand to touch her mother's tenderly.

"I will not fail you this time," she said with pride.

Vanessa looked her daughter up and down, evaluating if she were the best one to send for this job. She would have just done it herself, but she had other business that she needed to attend to. Between Nitra and Thad, they should be able to handle it.

Nitra waited expectantly for her mother to wish her well on her journey.

"Try your best not to let any of those ... humans see you," Vanessa said sternly to her.

Before she could release her shoulder, Nitra quickly replied, "Yes, Mother."

Chapter 9

Samhain

By the time I made it back to my house, I was soaking wet from the heavy rain. The weight of my clothes slowed me down, but at the same time, I couldn't have cared less. I kept reliving the last few hours over and over again in my head, reminding myself that I hadn't been dreaming.

Kailani and I had walked together from the party to her little cottage, which was located on a secluded part of the beach, on the southern end of the island. The front of the cozy home was nestled within a small cove that provided cover from the view of the surrounding houses. As we kissed goodbye in the rain, in this tiny nook of paradise, it felt like we were the only two people on the face of this earth.

Now that I had made it home, I noticed my aunt's Corvette was in the driveway. She'd left the porch light on for me, but the rest of the lights in the house were out. This late at night I assumed they were both asleep. However, I still found myself stopping in the upstairs hallway to peek into Alana's room, just to check to make sure that she was all right. I was relieved to see that she was sleeping soundly.

My own sleep did not come easily. I was still way too excited about how my evening had unfolded. I lay in my bed, tossing and turning for hours, already looking forward to the next time I would see Kailani again.

When I woke the next morning, well afternoon actually,

I was still on cloud nine. The sky remained overcast, but the storm had already passed. I found that even the gloomy weather couldn't dampen my spirits and I had to literally stop myself from skipping down the stairs two at a time.

I was thankful for my little bit of self control when I reached the bottom and saw Alana sitting on the couch, wrapped in a luxe blanket, still wearing her pajamas. Chocolate wrappers littered the floor all around her and she was sitting there, eating popcorn, watching some girly chick flick movie.

She looked at me with red, puffy eyes, then looked right back to the television screen. I came over and sat down beside her, but still she said nothing. Over the noise from the movie, I could hear Aunt Tess messing around in the kitchen, preparing our meal for that evening.

Finally, Alana spoke, "Jason and I broke up."

Her words came out just above a whisper.

"I figured," I said, eyeing the wrappers, my voice as sympathetic as I could manage.

"When I told him I didn't want to be with him any more after the way he acted, he told me he didn't really care and said that he never even liked me that much to begin with."

She choked out the last part as she had to take a shaky breath to fight back more tears.

"I'm so sorry."

When I spoke the words, I really meant them. As much as I hated Jason, I hated seeing my cousin like this even more. I wasn't sorry that they broke up, but furiously sorry that he was still hurting her.

"Don't be sorry," she said, "I'm the one who should be apologizing to you. I never should have gotten mad at you for punching him last night. I know you were only trying to look out for me. It was just, when I saw everyone staring at me," she let out an exasperated sigh, "well, everything seemed so different under the haze of embarrassment."

"Well, I'm sorry for embarrassing you, but I must admit, it did feel pretty darn good when my fist landed on his ugly face."

She managed to stifle a little laugh, then jerked her head up as if she had just remembered something.

"So, how did the party go last night?"

"It was all right," I said, trying to keep myself from smiling. "There was a blond boy there from our Physics class. He asked about you."

"Phillip?"

"I think that was his name. He seemed nice."

"Yeah, he is... he's just not really my type."

"Oh, really! And what exactly is your type? Crazy? Jealous? Controlling?" I asked her sarcastically.

"Stop!" she cried as she broke out with a real smile this time, pushing hard against my shoulder with her hands.

The noises that were coming from the kitchen kept getting louder and louder. Alana looked over to me. "I think we should go offer to help Mom. It sounds like things are getting a little frantic in there."

Aunt Tess wouldn't allow us to help her with the meal. It was one of her many superstitions that only the cook was allowed to touch the food. She did, however, instruct us to go set the table in the dining room. Everything she gave us, from the tablecloths to the napkins, plates, cups and candles, were black.

She also requested that tonight, for dinner, we dress head to toe, in the exact same shade. It was kind of creepy, but I had to admit it went along perfectly with the evening's strange monochromatic dinner theme.

After everything was set up and ready to go, I went upstairs to take a shower. Once I had finished and gotten myself dressed, I tried calling Kailani's house several times, but I couldn't ever get anyone to answer. I reasoned that maybe, because it was almost time for the dinner to begin, she had already left.

The doorbell rang and I almost ran down the stairs before I heard a man's voice speak a greeting as someone opened the door for him. I assumed that this had to be Rick, Tess's boyfriend. He was also supposed to be joining us for dinner tonight, where I was going to be meeting him for the first time.

Tess had instructed everyone to be at the bottom of the stairs at precisely nine and I glanced at the clock, not wanting to arrive a minute too soon. The only thing that actually made me want to come down was knowing that Kailani would also be arriving soon and I didn't want her to feel uncomfortable, being down there, alone with everybody.

As I walked down the stairs, gripping the iron railing, I saw that everyone was dressed in their appropriate black attire. Rick was in an expensive looking suit and Alana and Tess were both wearing long, flowing skirts. To me it looked as if they were all ready to go to a funeral. From the few things that I'd heard about tonight's dinner, I guessed, in a way, we kind of were.

Rick introduced himself with a firm handshake. His

greasy, black hair was slicked back with way too much gel and his dark, beady eyes were intense and scrutinizing as I returned the handshake, telling him my name.

I felt the tingling begin, just before the doorbell rang again and I excused myself, thankful for the relief from the tense moment. I opened the door, expecting to see Kailani, but it was Liam and Kat instead. They were dressed up like two of the vampires from those popular movies. Their golden eyes were glowing and their skin was pale with an eerie perfection.

"Trick or treat!" they sang in unison.

"Oh! Hi guys. Happy Halloween!" I said, reaching for the green plastic bowl by the door to give them both some candy.

"Kailani couldn't make it," Kat told me with a small frown.

"Our grandmother asked her to go and help with some last minute errands. They had to go out of town so she won't be back until Tuesday. She said for me to come and tell you, since she didn't have time to call. She also said to tell you that she was sorry for the last minute cancellation."

"Oh, that's okay," I said, trying not to sound too disappointed, "You guys can come in if you'd like. We were just about to sit down to have dinner."

Kat was already shaking her head no, when Liam poked his head through the door.

"What's on the menu?" he asked as he breathed in the wonderful aroma that was now flooding in from the kitchen.

I hesitated, realizing that I didn't even know.

"Let me just ask my aunt. I'm sure she won't mind if you join us."

I figured that she wouldn't, especially since one of our expected guests, unexpectedly wouldn't be coming. Kat and

Liam were already here, but I still wanted to give Aunt Tess the courtesy of asking.

Of course she said she didn't mind. There was plenty of food to go around.

After setting the dining room table for an additional guest, I walked back into the foyer, where everyone stood, quietly waiting. Tess then asked me to hang the "DO NOT DISTURB" sign on the front door of the house and turn out the front porch light.

After I'd done that, she began to give everyone the history and instructions for tonight's dinner. Her voice had become deep and solemn.

"As many of you know, Halloween has long been said to be the one night a year where the veil that separates the world of the living from the world of the dead is at its all time thinnest. Most people believe that is why it is then possible for the spirits to penetrate that veil in order to communicate with the world of the living." She paused for dramatic effect.

"As Pagans, we celebrate Halloween a little differently than most Americans. To us, it is known as Samhain, or the Fire Festival. It is celebrated in many ways, but one of those ways is to have a Dumb Supper, also known to some as the Feast of the Dead. It is done in remembrance of our beloved ancestors and friends who have already completed their life's journey and passed on to the other side. The dinner is always served in complete silence, from the moment you enter the dining room, until we all stand together to exit. This is done in the hopes that you will then open your hearts, minds and ears so that the deceased may be heard, should they wish to communicate."

I glanced over at Liam and Kat to make sure they didn't seem too weirded out by all of this nonsense. However, they seemed genuinely intrigued and were concentrating intently on Tess's words as if they were studying them. They nodded along as Tess spoke. The only one who seemed uninterested, bored even, was Rick. He kept glancing down to check the time on his Rolex.

Tess continued her instructions, "The spirit chair, at the head of the table, is shrouded in a black cloth and is left empty for our 'guest' or 'guests of honor.' I have placed photos of both of my grandparents in front of the chair, but if any of you have loved ones whom you would like to invite, please say a quick prayer, asking them to join us."

Tess reached over and grabbed a stack of steno pads and pens by the door.

"Here. Take these and write down a message that you would like to send to your guest. At the end of the meal we will burn the papers in a candle's flame so that, as the smoke rises, our messages will be delivered to the other side. Also, just so you know, this meal is traditionally served backwards, starting with the dessert."

At this, I saw Liam look excitedly over at Kat, as if saying "See. Aren't you glad that we stayed?"

Once we were all seated in the dining room, we sat in complete silence as we enjoyed a warm Apple Betty with whipped cream and coffee. The room was dim and we would have been in complete darkness if it weren't for a few black candles on the table, which created a faint glow, barely illuminating the food.

The main course for dinner was a Chicken Hawthorne

stuffed breast with forest mushroom gravy along with a side of asparagus and a baked potato. This was followed by a pumpkin butternut squash soup and a fresh garden salad. It somehow surprised me to discover that my aunt was such a great cook.

After our meal was over, Tess cleared our dishes, then took her paper in hand and walked over to the spirit chair. She briefly placed her hand on each of the black picture frames that held the photos of her deceased grandparents. She put the paper up close to her heart then closed her eyes in prayer. After a minute she moved the paper over the flame of the candle until it lit, placed it in a stone basin then watched as it went up in smoke.

She returned to her seat and placed her hand on Rick's shoulder to signify that it was his turn.

While I watched each guest go up to the head of the table, I couldn't help but glance nervously at the dark chair looming there, wondering if some spirit was occupying it silently. When at last it was my turn, I tentatively got up and walked over to the chair.

I looked down at the old pictures on the table of my great-grandparents. These were relatives that I had never even met. Their grave expressions looked creepy in the flickering candlelight. I guess no one ever smiled back in those days, I thought as I recalled every old photograph that I had ever seen.

I held out my folded piece of paper to the flame and watched as it slowly began to burn. Out of the corner of my eye I saw a translucent mist start to materialize, as if someone were sitting there in the chair. My hand hovered over the basin as the temperature in the room seemed to drop instantaneously. I felt chilling goose bumps go up and down my arms and neck.

What felt like an ice cold hand reached out to grab my arm. I dropped the paper as the fire then reached my fingertips. The candles flickered for a moment, then extinguished simultaneously, leaving the room in complete and total darkness.

Abruptly, a man's voice spoke three words through the air of the dark room.

"Beware. Danger. Tiwaz."

His words were choppy, as if it were an immense struggle for him to get them out.

The grip on my arm was suddenly gone, as was our brief visitor, but my arm stayed frozen, along with the rest of my body. Shock continued to course through me from his unexpected message. It wasn't the man's words, however that had me transfixed and terrified. It was his voice.

It had seemed so emotional, as he seemed so determined to get through, so desperate for his message to be heard. His voice was so familiar that I felt my stomach drop, praying that it couldn't be him.

Please don't let it be him, I whispered to myself.

At the same time, there was no doubt in my mind whose voice this was. This was the voice of a friend, the voice of kind advice, the voice of comfort. This was a voice that I had grown up all of my life listening to, a voice that told me numerous stories at bedtime.

This voice I knew as well as my own. It was my father's.

Chapter 10

Haunted

The dinner was over for me immediately.

Trying to stay calm, I walked slowly out of the dining room, then ran up the stairs to my room and went straight for my cell phone. I tried calling my dad's house several times, but the phone just rang and rang with no answer.

Filled with dread, I then tried my grandparent's house and when my grandmother finally answered the phone, I could tell by her voice that she had been crying. At first she tried to act as if nothing were wrong, for my sake.

But then, hesitantly, when I asked, she confirmed my worst fear.

She said that she had received a call about an hour earlier from her friend John. He was the Captain there at Kenai's local Fire Department. She said all of the information hadn't been released yet, but he told her that there had been an accident aboard the crab boat that my father had been working on and somehow, my dad had slipped and fallen overboard into the icy waters.

She told me that one of his shipmates had witnessed him fall and tried to save him. The man said it was almost as if my dad had simply disappeared as soon as he hit the dark water. The crew and then rescue workers had searched for hours, yet were never able to recover his body.

While I was still on the phone with grandma and she

was telling me everything she knew, I felt someone quietly let themselves into my room, I assumed to check on me. But with my mind in such complete disarray and being transfixed on my grandmother's every word, I wasn't paying them much attention.

After getting off the phone, I realized that whoever it was, was now gone and I couldn't even begin to guess who it had been.

I lay down in my bed, huddled under the covers as if they might bring me some small comfort, but after hearing the devastating news there was no way I could sleep. I remained restless for most of the night as I lye awake, wishing there was something I could do, yet knowing for certain that there was nothing.

In the wee hours of the morning, I finally began to drift in and out of consciousness. Whenever I would fall asleep, I kept having the same dream over and over. I was onboard a ship, holding onto my dad's hand as he dangled over the side. As hard as I tried to hold on to his icy fingers, he just kept slipping out of my grasp, inevitably plunging into the cold, dark waters below.

The next day I never left my room.

A soft knock on my bedroom door Monday morning woke me and I opened my eyes to realize that the morning had arrived. The grey light of dawn was flooding in through my balcony door window. Coming out of the sleepy fog in my head, I heard the door crack, then slowly open before I heard someone's voice whisper hoarsely.

"Hey. How are you?"

It was Alana.

"Fine," I lied, sitting up in my bed groggily, unwilling to make eye contact with her.

"I'm so sorry!" she said in a slightly louder voice, quickly crossing the room before she enveloped me a tight hug.

She sat down on the bed beside me and burrowed her head into the crook of my neck. Her hysterical sobs let me know just how upset she really was. Brogan had, after all, been her only uncle.

It was strange. Even though I felt completely dead inside, I also felt a calming strength radiating from within me. I found myself stroking Alana's hair, trying to comfort her, when it should have been the other way around. When she finally stopped crying, Alana looked up at me.

"Mom isn't taking the news very well either. After she spoke to grandma the other night, I could hear her crying in her room all night long."

I now had a vague recollection of handing Aunt Tess the phone after I had finished speaking. Or did she take it from my non-responsive hand? As I was trying to remember, Alana continued to talk.

"She told me that she thought it would be best if you took the day off from school. I told her that I would stay home with you -- that I wanted to stay with you -- but she insisted I give you some time to yourself."

Alana paused, perhaps hoping that this would turn into a conversation, not just a monologue. When I offered her no cooperation, she continued on her own.

"I'll talk to the principal for you. I'm sure he'll understand your absence. He might even excuse you from your punishment."

Now, on top of everything else, I remembered that had happened too. I'd totally forgotten about it.

"Oh. Thanks," I told her in an empty, hollow voice that even I didn't recognize.

She wiped her eyes with the backs of her hands and kissed me on the cheek.

"Try to get some rest," she told me before hurrying out the door.

After watching the door close behind her, I lay back down. I felt numb. I started staring at the stars that decorated my ceiling and listening to the sounds in the house as I heard Tess and Alana getting ready to leave for work and school.

Somehow, after or during this time, I must have fallen back asleep.

I could tell because the nightmare was back, although this time it was slightly different. This time, right before my father fell to his death, he looked up at me and his expression turned from fear to concern.

"Use Tiwaz," he told me.

Then he reached up with his free hand, right before slipping from my fingers. I watched, horrified and completely helpless, as he fell through the air.

This time, when he hit the water, I saw a strange, metallic flash of red and gold, just under the surface, right there beside him. He sank quickly beneath the rough waves that were littered with chunks of floating ice and I saw the strange, golden-crimson creature follow.

I watched them both for as long as I could, but the second I blinked they were gone.

I woke with a start and looked over at the lit up red

numbers on my alarm clock. It was already 11:05 am. I lay there in the bed for a while longer, continuing to think about the unsettling dream and remembering those same flashes of similar colors from the beach, my last night in Alaska.

This time the creature had been closer, so I had been able to see more details on it. I'd seen its large tail as it dove deeper after my father and now knew for sure that it was some kind of fish. Its metallic scales were the size of quarters and that was what was reflecting the light.

I decided to get on my computer and do some research to see if I could figure out exactly what type of piscine creature this was. Then another thought came to my mind. I also really needed to find out what the word Tiwaz meant. I'd heard my father use it twice now.

I signed on to my account and heard the familiar message "You've got mail."

I then checked my inbox and realized there were several messages sent from Abby. I scrolled down for a moment before clicking on the first.

From:abigailthomas@yahoo.com
Subject: WORRIED!!! PLEASE RESPOND!!!
Date: Oct 31, 2015.10:05pm
To:adenwilder@aol.com

Dear Aden,

OMG, I'm sooo sorry!!! Your grandmother called me as soon as she got off the phone with Tess. She told me what happened. I tried to call your cell phone, but it went straight to voice mail. How are you? Are you doing OK? I can fly down ASAP if you need me to. Please respond as soon as you get this or call me! I'm really worried and just want to talk to you. I miss you so much!!!

Love, Abby.

I walked over to my phone on the night stand and saw that the power was off. Tess must have done it the other night, while she was in here. Whether it was an accident or deliberate, I didn't know. After taking a moment to power back on, it showed me that I had four missed calls, all of which were from Abby. I scrolled down to her number and was about to hit the dial button when a loud honk, from outside the house, startled me so much that I jumped. I walked out onto my balcony and saw a bright red Lamborghini parked in the driveway. Leaning against the passenger door was a girl with long, dark, straight hair that resembled black silk. She was propped up against the car by the sole of one of her knee-high, black leather boots.

This girl on her own was already smoking hot, but with the combination of the designer car behind her, she was practically combustible.

Her arms were crossed in front of her defiantly, but when she noticed me come out, she lifted her dark sunglasses and smiled exultantly. Her bright, red, painted lips were turned up on the edges and their vivid color matched her form fitting tank top, which stood out in contrast to her dark, olive-tanned skin.

"Hey! Come down. I need your help!" she yelled up at me with a wave.

I just stared at her for a minute, racking my brain for any recollection of who she might be. I had nothing.

I then found myself turning back to my room and heading out the door so I could go down to meet her. As I was descending the stairs, a small voice inside my head kept whispering a warning, telling me not to go. I kept thinking to myself, what am I doing? I don't even know this girl and here I am doing as she says without even asking any questions.

Even so, I couldn't stop my feet from moving, one in front of the other. I opened the front door and strolled down the sidewalk. The closer I got to her, the more I could feel that strange tingling sensation that I had gotten so used to with Kailani, Kat and Liam.

Now though, it felt slightly different. Painfully different. Dangerously different.

Her smile widened with my approach and her large, brown doe eyes sparkled. As soon as I was within reaching distance, she grabbed my hand.

"Why, hello handsome," she purred in a soft silky voice as she gently stroked my palm.

"I'm Nitra."

She paused, raking me up and down with her eyes before continuing.

"I was just on my way to St. Petersburg, but somehow I must have gotten lost."

Clumsily I introduced myself then started to give her directions.

Before I could even finish my first sentence though, she interrupted me, "Well, you see, I'm not from around here. Obviously."

She ran her other hand down her body as if she were inviting me to look at what she was wearing.

"I really don't know anyone and I'm terrible at directions, so surely I will get lost."

She ran her finger teasingly down my right shoulder.

"You seem like a nice guy, extremely good-looking, trustworthy. Is there anyway I could talk you into going with me? You know, just to show me the way?"

Her voice was so enticing, but alarms were going off in the back of my mind, warning me to say no. I could hear the voice inside my head again, telling me not to go, only this time it was louder.

"Um...well, actually I was just about to..."

She grabbed both of my hands and firmly curled them into hers as she pulled me closer.

"Please," she pouted, giving me the sad, puppy dog face.

I found myself staring at the gold flakes that were speckled in her exotic, chocolate brown eyes. I was now absolutely hypnotized by the magnetic current that I felt flowing between us.

Seeing that I was still considering, she quickly added, "I could really use an attractive, yet competent navigator."

She pulled me in even closer.

I managed a smile and somehow convinced myself that maybe she wasn't so dangerous after all.

"I guess I could ride with you, just for a little while."

Obviously pleased, she then dropped both of my hands.

"Good," she said, turning to walk around the car.

I looked down at the ground for a second, trying to clear my mind. A thought then occurred to me.

"When would you be able to bring me back?"

She flashed me a wicked grin before sliding into driver's seat.

"Whenever you wish."

She reached over and opened the passenger door and I got in and sank down into the black leather of the Lamborghini. Looking over at her, I noticed that her leather mini skirt had become even shorter now that she was sitting down in the car.

I tried to make myself stop staring.

"Where are you from?" I asked her, as we pulled out of the driveway.

"The West Coast," she replied elusively.

I waited for her to say more, but she just sat there staring straight ahead. She suddenly seemed as if she were lost in deep thought so I looked through my darkly tinted window, out at the gloomy day. I could see the winds were starting to pick up and the palm trees had begun to oscillate as we started driving off the island.

I began looking around the inside of the car, my eyes scanning the interior features and checking out all of the amenities this sweet ride had to offer.

When I looked back at Nitra, she remained awfully quiet and seemed to now be obsessively focused on her driving. I wished that she would say something to me, just to help ease this anxious feeling that I had building in the pit of my stomach.

I interrupted the uncomfortable silence as we drove, instructing her as to which direction she needed to go, but she remained silent, staring intently out the windshield.

Finally, as we approached the Sunshine Skyway Bridge, she began humming along with a song on the radio. I listened attentively to her voice, entranced by the sound of the hypnotic melody, and I started to feel a little calmer.

Once we were actually on the bridge, I looked down to the surface of the emerald green waters, way below in the gulf. They receded even further away as we continued to climb higher and higher.

When we arrived at the crest of the overpass, I noticed a young girl in a grey hoodie up ahead, standing on my side of the road. She was up on the ledge and was staring down at the ocean far below us.

"Stop the car!" I yelled over to Nitra.

She pulled over onto the easement, screeching to a stop. There was barely enough room for the car. Thankfully, the doors of the Lamborghini opened upward and not outward, so I was able to easily snake my way out.

I ran over and jumped up on the ledge beside the frightened girl, trying not to scare her in the process. An overwhelming scent of gasoline wafted through the air and I began to feel dizzy.

"Please don't do this," I begged her, trying my best to keep a calm, soothing tone as I offered her my hand.

She looked through me with her sad, lifeless eyes before she suddenly turned, then jumped.

I lunged forward to try to grab her, but I was too late. I fell to my knees to keep myself from losing balance and as I looked down, I saw her fall for several seconds. Her arms and legs flailed through the air and to me it felt as if my heart were falling with her.

Then the strangest thing happened. When she was about halfway down, her body suddenly disappeared into thin air.

I continued to stare at the empty space where I had last seen her, moments before. I was hoping for...what? Even I didn't know.

Nitra startled me by propping her hands up on the three and a half foot concrete wall that I was now lying on. I was still looking down at the choppy waters below, trying to make sense of what just happened. The gusty winds were mounting and the suspension bridge had begun to sway slightly, making me feel even sicker.

"You know she wasn't real," Nitra stated calmly.

I looked at her with a vacant expression.

"Do you know how many people have died on this bridge?" she asked, then waited for a moment.

"Hundreds. Mostly suicides," she replied after I had looked away and didn't answer.

As I lay on the cool concrete, I caught another strong whiff of gasoline drifting through the air. For a second, panic began to set in. I began thinking that maybe there was something wrong with Nitra's car, but when I looked back, everything seemed intact.

Nitra saw me looking back at the car and she took a deep, indulgent breath, as if she were enjoying the smell of the gas.

"They say this bridge is haunted by the ghosts of the victims, from all of the tragedies that have happened here," she said.

She leaned out over the edge, looking straight down, and continued her story.

"Did you know that from here, it's almost a seventeen-story drop. It only takes three to four seconds before impact. You'd hit the water at roughly seventy-five miles an hour."

I looked over at her, wondering how she could be so nonchalant. She almost seemed quietly pleased about all the tragedies that had happened here. She continued looking down, never noticing the way that I was gaping at her. She just kept going with her story.

"Most people die instantly from the impact as they hit the water. They break their necks, rupture organs. Some live on for a few minutes, before they eventually drown, unable to swim back to the surface."

Her voice stayed calm and soothing, but her words were cruel and heartless. When she finally looked up and over at me, I saw that she had begun to smile maliciously. She reached over, placing the palm of her hand on my back.

"Jump Aden," she whispered in a crooning hiss.

Her words had put me into a trancelike state and it took me a few seconds before I realized what she was asking me to do.

"You can be with your father again," she cooed to me, making the decision to jump somehow sound appealing.

Wait! How did she know about my father?

The wind was now howling around me and whipping my hair into my eyes. I suddenly felt as if I had a very heavy weight on my chest, overwhelming me with sadness and pulling me down. Not only was my sorrow for my dad, but also for all of the others who had lost their lives, suffering so much here on this bridge.

I thought about how I'd never be able to see my father again, never get to say goodbye. It was just unbearable.

My mind then went to all of my friends back home who had promised to write or call, but never did. It made me question if they were ever really my friends at all. I thought about my mother, who didn't want me, abandoning me to grow up without her.

I tried not to, but then I couldn't help thinking about Kailani, promising me that she would come to dinner, but then not showing up. She could be so wishy-washy sometimes, I thought. Hot one moment, then cold the next. I wasn't even sure how she really felt about me. I began to wonder if I was just wasting my time. Why wouldn't she have just called me to cancel our plans herself?

Slowly I sat up on the ledge, letting my legs dangle over the edge. I thought about how easy it would be to just give up, give in to the sorrow which was now causing my entire body to feel so heavy.

I could still feel Nitra's hand resting on my back. My skin was prickling at her touch as the heat from her fingers kept growing. It almost felt like there was fire coming from her hand, starting to burn me.

Defeated, I closed my eyes and prepared to push myself off the edge. I tired to picture Kailani's face one last time. As I did this, I felt as if I could somehow feel her presence and this gave me another ray of hope.

A newfound strength came over me and I knew that I had to see her again. I had to find out for myself what really happened with her. How selfish would it be of me to just give up? Leaving behind my family and friends, like Abby and Alana, wouldn't they suffer from the consequences of my actions?

I looked behind me, to Nitra.

"I can't do it," I told her.

Confusion clouded her features, but only for a second.

"You don't have a choice," she said angrily.

Her hand was now so hot that it was scalding my skin. I winced from the pain and pulled away, but before I could move out of her reach, with an unbelievable force she pushed me over the edge.

I flew outward, several feet from the bridge before I began to drop, my stomach jumping up to my heart. As gravity took over, I began to fall faster and faster.

An unexpected gust of wind sent me flying backward and rotated me from my upright position, causing me to look straight down at the dark waters below. It was as if they were calling up to me, taunting me. They appeared so cold and uninviting, yet ultimately inescapable.

As the waves of the surface seemed to race up toward me, I thought to myself, this is it. I stiffly braced myself for the impact.

When I hit the water, I hit hard. The impact was so violent that it felt as if my head had been ripped off my neck. I tried to use my arms and legs to swim to the surface, but I quickly realized I couldn't move. I no longer had any control over my body. I began to panic as I ran out of oxygen, sinking deeper and deeper into the dark ocean. I could see the sunlight above gradually getting dimmer as I continued to sink.

As I looked above me, in my peripheral vision I noticed a familiar glint of metallic red and orange scales, rapidly closing in on me. I thought to myself, why would that peculiar ornate fish from the beach be here?

For a second I let myself believe that it was actually going to help me, as I felt a pair of female arms wrap around my chest from behind. However, instead of pulling me to the surface, as I had hoped, they only dragged me deeper. I tried to struggle against them but it was useless.

Besides the fact that I was paralyzed from the neck down, this thing was way too strong and fast. Unlike me, she was perfectly acclimated to the underwater world. The last thing I remember before my vision went completely black was looking up at the small circle of sunlight, which now seemed so far away.

Slowly it began to fade, along with my last hopes of rescue.

Chapter 11
Kailani

*K*ailani dragged Aden's lifeless body up onto the beach and into the cove, in front of her cottage. The whole time she had been taking him home, she'd been holding his head up, above the water, praying that he would miraculously take a breath, but it never happened.

The other night, Kailani had been talking privately with her grandmother, when she received a message from Kat, telling her what had happened to Aden at the dinner party. When Kat told her about his father, Kailani decided to cut her visit short and head back home the next day.

Kailani shared an extraordinary connection with her twin sister. They could communicate with each other telepathically, even at vast distances, above or below the water. Most of their kind, without being able to exchange words with each other under the water, needed physical contact.

When Kat contacted Kailani again this morning and told her that Aden hadn't shown up for class, she figured that he had just stayed home in mourning. At the same time she realized that she was unable to put to rest this eerie feeling she had that something else was going on. This unease spurred her on to return home even faster.

Aden hadn't been hard for Kailani to find. The strange fact that he radiated some type of magnetic energy made it easy. It was kind of like the gravitational force that becomes stronger the closer you get to the earth's core. The strength of his pulling intensified the closer that she got to him. It was like a beacon.

She had talked to her sister about it before, but while Kat said that she and Liam could also feel it slightly, at close distances, she admitted that it was nowhere near as strong and intense as Kailani described it.

Kailani remembered being completely confused as she felt herself being led to the iconic bridge. From a distance, she looked up from the sea, searching for him. She began to feel a mounting sense of urgency. A fleeting moment of relief came when she finally saw his face, peering down at the water from the top of the bridge, but it quickly then turned to concern.

Why would he be sitting up there all alone, so high on the ledge? she wondered.

She soon realized the peril he was in, as well as the fact that she had arrived too late, when she saw her cousin, Nitra, standing there behind him. Helplessly she watched as Nitra callously shoved him off of the bridge.

Kailani tried to then break his fall by sending out a massive gust of wind, which blasted him backward. She realized that this had also notified Nitra of her arrival when she saw Nitra quickly jump into the water after him.

When Kailani reached the place in the water where they had landed, she found Nitra dragging Aden down toward the bottom of the ocean. Rage and panic swelled inside Kailani, commingling with equal intensity.

If the impact alone hadn't killed him, he would need air, soon. Desperate to save him, Kailani tried to pull Nitra away from Aden. She hadn't realized, at the time, that Thad, Nitra's personal bodyguard, was there as well.

Appearing out of nowhere, he pulled Kailani away with his huge, strong hands and no matter how hard she tried, struggling continuously against him, she could not break free.

The anguish that Kailani felt as she helplessly watched Aden being dragged even deeper made her vision hazy. She was outnumbered and completely out of options.

Sudden her sister's voice was there inside her head.

"We're here," Kat told her.

Before Kailani could even look around, her hands were freed as Liam wrestled Thad away.

Kailani quickly descended toward Nitra and Aden to see that her sister was already there, trying to fight off Nitra. Kailani wrapped her hands around her cousin's face, digging her fingernails deep into her cheeks and eyes, pulling her head back at the same time.

Kat had Nitra's tail and was twisting it as if she were trying to wring out a dishcloth. Finally Nitra let go, shrieking in pain as she retreated from the fight.

As soon as Aden was free, Kailani, her sister and Liam all used their powers collectively to create massive undercurrents that swept the intruders futher away.

Before they had been carried out very far by the undercurrent, Kailani watched Thad's body being swept into some large rocks nearby. Immediately he disintegrated into sea foam.

Kat and Liam then took off after Nitra, when they knew they had created enough distance between her and Kailani and Aden.

Kailani wondered briefly if Thad's fate would also be bestowed upon Nitra or if her cousin would somehow manage to escape. Still fueled by anger, she decided that at this moment she really didn't care. Right now that was the least of her worries. Using all of the strength she had left, Kailani recovered Aden's abandoned body.

Deep in the dark water, he was floating face down, not moving at all. By the way his head was bent to the side, she was quite sure that his neck was broken. Heartbroken, she desperately tried to pull him back up to the surface as quickly as she could.

Hope began to fuel her on even faster when she realized that she could still feel the warmth inside him. She could also feel that same tingling sensation that always accompanied his touch. She hurried to get him above the water, now clinging on to new hope, when just minutes before all had seemed hopeless.

On the way up, one question kept nagging at Kailani. Why had Nitra seemed so desperate to kill Aden?

She pushed the thought aside to revisit it later. At the moment she needed to focus all of her energy on getting him back to the air so that he could breathe.

When they broke the surface, he did not start breathing. She tried to breathe air back into his lungs. Still nothing.

It had seemed like forever but she finally got him back to her home and dragged his body up onto the beach. She gently placed his head on the sand, but was discouraged because he had still not taken one breath.

She'd taken a CPR class about a year earlier and decided that even though it had now been too long since he'd had any oxygen, it was still worth a try.

She looked down at his perfectly shaped lips. They were cold and blue. She placed her mouth tightly on his as she tried to breathe life back into his unresponsive lungs.

"I'm so sorry," she told him as she used her own body weight to push against his chest. "This is all my fault!"

She kept apologizing as she alternated pushing against his chest then blowing air into his lungs. After repeating the process way too many times, she began to realize that it was useless.

She brushed the damp, dark hair out of his closed eyes. This reminded her of how beautiful his silvery-grey eyes were, eyes that she would never again be able to look into. She thought about the way they used to look at her. This thought was unbearable.

Her fingers lingered on Aden's cheek as she stared at his relaxed face, trying to remember every time they had kissed.

She suddenly realized that she was still able to experience that tingling sensation, but she now knew that she had mistakenly believed that it had been tied to his life force. She leaned down to kiss him one last time.

"I really did love you," she whispered to deaf ears.

With her eyes closed tightly, she turned away. It was just too painful to see him broken this way.

She had never before been this sad in her entire life. She now wished that she could cry, that she could at least shed one tear over her first true love. He deserved at least that.

But it was impossible. Mermaids could not cry, for they had no tears. It was just one of the subtle reminders that their souls, unlike a human's, were not immortal.

Suddenly she felt a hand touch her arm.

Startled, her whole body jerked and she turned back around to find Aden sitting there, upright, beside her. His intense, beautiful eyes were full of life and they were now locked on hers.

Reaching up with both hands, he rested each of his palms on her cheeks. Slowly and gently he pulled her face to his.

Right before he kissed her, he said, "I love you too, Kailani." His smile was warm and radiant.

His voice sounded scratchy, yet firm, and the emotion in his words matched Kailani's own. Her heart jumped a beat hearing him call her by her real name. Overwhelmed and breathless she was unable to control her excitement as she pulled back from him for a second.

"You're here!" she exclaimed, "You're alive! But how?"

She realized that it didn't matter. She kissed him again, pulling him to her. Feeling like she couldn't get close enough, she instinctively tried to crawl up into his lap before she remembered that at the moment she didn't have her legs.

She watched as his gaze dropped to her iridescent tail. The sun was glinting reflectively off her metallic scales. They appeared turquoise one second, then lavender the next, as her muscles undulated beneath them. She had always thought that him seeing her like this would make her self-conscious, but after everything they had just been through, all she felt was relief.

"Well, I guess now you know my secret," she said.

She sighed as she glanced down and began brushing the sand off her tail. Only dead air greeted her statement. She sat there for a moment, waiting for him to say something, anything.

After a while he still had not said anything and her confidence began to waver. She decided to speak again.

"I know it's a lot to take in. Do you think that it's weird?" she asked, glancing over to find him smiling at her in wonder.

"No. I don't. I think it's the most beautiful and amazing thing I've ever seen in my life. How could I ever be weirded out by anything that was a part of you?"

He paused and she saw his smile falter a bit and his eyes begin to crinkle as if he were suddenly lost in a deep thought. He looked away before he could ask his next question.

"What I don't understand is why you were trying to keep this a secret? When did this happen?"

At first she did not understand. She felt just as confused as he seemed to be. She searched his face for a moment before finally realizing that he probably thought this was the real reason she did not come to his dinner the other night.

"This didn't just happen, Aden. This is how I was born, it's what I really am."

He looked back at her with questioning eyes.

Knowing that she no longer had a choice, she decided to go ahead and explain everything to him. She took a moment to first try to decide where she should begin.

"Do you remember our summer reading project? The story we reviewed in our World Literature class, our first day of school?"

His blank stare told her that he did not.

"The one about The Little Mermaid?" *she prompted.*

Slowly he began to nod, a hint of recognition now showing on his face.

"Well, her name was Calyssa. She was my grandmother's youngest sister."

He still looked confused. It took him a minute to process this information before he began to speak.

"But I thought that story was written sometime back in the 1800's. Wouldn't that make your grandmother like…"

"Two hundred years old? Yes." *Kailani answered, before he could do the math. She kept her expression grave and remained silent for a moment to let him accept this fact. She knew that he would have a lot more questions for her now.*

After several seconds of his silence, the questions began.

"If you really are a mermaid, then how is it that you grow legs to walk upon the land?"

She could tell that he really did believe her now, even if what he said came out a little more skeptically than he had meant it to.

"Right before my grandmother's father died, he gave her a special sapphire. By using its powers, she created a potion that gives the Mer who consumes it a temporary human form. As long as we continue to drink a sip of it every few hours, we will remain in that form."

Kailani thought about leaving it at that, but then decided to explain things to him just a little bit more.

"All Mer are born with the ability to manipulate the element of water. It is a power that is connected and deeply embedded in our DNA. Over the years, as we get older, we are taught to control it. The sapphire that my grandmother possesses, the one used to make the potion, also harnesses the powers of Aeolus, the Greek god of wind. As a side effect, all who drink it can also manipulate this element."

Aden was then quiet for several minues. Kailani assumed that he was remembering the incident at the gym, as well as that day at the lunch table. She sat there, patiently waiting for him to process it all.

"What about the girl? The one with the black hair?" Aden then asked her, "Nitra. The one who tried to kill me?"

Kailani's face hardened at this reminder and her voice came out far more steely than she had intended it to.

"She is one of my cousins from the Pacific Kingdom. Her mother, Vanessa, is one of my grandmother's sisters. She's the second oldest."

Kailani saw that Aden was now watching her intently, hooked on every word that she was saying, as she continued her story.

"Nitra's father is a Selkie, which means that even though her tail looks similar to her mother's, she really is a hybrid. She's capable of going in and out of the ocean at will, without having to rely on a potion. She can remain human on land as long as she keeps herself dry."

He nodded as if all of this made complete sense to him.

"But why did she want me to kill myself?" he asked, "While we were on the bridge, she told me to jump."

Kailani was puzzled because she recalled him being pushed. She looked away, staring out at the ocean, unable to look him in the eye as she told him the gruesome details of her cousin's heritage.

"Vanessa, the Pacific Queen, as well as her family and most of her subjects, all hate humans. They believe themselves to be superior in every way, except one. For this reason they are constantly looking for ways to enable themselves to steal human souls. I've even heard rumors that there are some who reside over in the Pacific, who have taken up the ancient practice of the Sirens."

Figuring that he might not know who the Sirens were, she swallowed hard before choosing to go on.

"The Sirens would drown fisherman and sailors. They would then extract their bones, blood and organs. They would then use those remains to create very powerful, yet dangerous potions. Because of the violent way these potions are made, with the use of such dark magic, those who consume them would often find themselves suffering in constant pain. Trina, the sea witch that gave Calyssa the drought, which made her human, knew this. She was the most feared and powerful Siren of them all."

Kailani turned back to Aden to see how he was taking this latest news and watched as the color drained from his face. She knew Kat was now back at the cottage so she mentally sent her sister a message, asking her to bring him out a bottle of water.

For a few moments Aden did not say anything else. Kailani thought that maybe he might be in shock, but then she saw him suddenly snap out of it, as if he had just remembered something.

"When Nitra's hand was on my back, her touch was so hot that it was burning me."

He lifted the back of his wet t-shirt to show her where Nitra had touched him and Kailani could see that her cousin's hand print was scalded into his skin. The damage was pretty severe. It had to be at least a second or third degree burn.

Kailani's jaw clenched defensively with anger and she took a deep breath, trying to calm herself before explaining the reason that this had happened to him.

"Nitra's mother, Vanessa, was given a ruby at the same time my grandmother received her sapphire. Her ruby holds the power of Hephaestus, the fire god. What Vanessa has created, using its power allows the recipients to create underwater volcanic eruptions and boil water as well as burn another with their touch, among other things."

"So if your grandmother and Vanessa have stones with special powers, does that mean that all of the other sisters do too?"

"Yes. At one time the stones were all united. It was back when each of the sisters lived together in the Atlantic palace. On their father's death bed he gave them each a stone, explaining that it was no longer safe to keep them together. He asked each of his daughters, now that they were old enough, to take them and spread them out. Each of them then went on to rule one of the five oceanic kingdoms. He made them solemnly vow to do everything in their power to protect these stones, telling them what a huge responsibility it was and explaining the devastating consequences that could occur if they were to ever fall into the wrong hands."

Aden nodded acceptingly. He acted like he wanted to ask her more about this, but he had another question on his mind.

"Why do you think Nitra was following me?"

"Following you?"

"Yeah, I think it was her that I saw from a distance on the beach, my last night in Alaska."

The possibility that Nitra might have been specifically targeting him worried Kailani, but she tried not to show how much this alarmed her. Slowly she took another breath as she felt the sun come out to warm her back as the clouds began to clear.

"I'm sorry. I really don't know the answer to that question."

Aden stared at her for a moment then gave her one of his curious, yet adorably lop-sided grins.

"Your skin has lightened up two shades in the past couple of minutes. Why is that?" he asked her.

Kailani smiled, relieved to be answering such an easier question now.

"That's simple enough. The Mer are not warm blooded like humans. Our bodies are unable to maintain a regular temperature like yours can. We are cold-blooded, so we adapt to whatever our surroundings are at the time. When it is cool, our skin darkens so that we are able to absorb more of the light and heat. When it is warm outside, our skin lightens enabling us to reflect the rays of the sun."

Aden nodded that he understood and Kailani could see that he was putting the pieces together, absorbing all of this new information like a sponge.

"Is there anything else you can do? Any other special powers," he asked her.

Kailani could see how intrigued he was, but she had to swallow hard before finally answering. She was suddenly afraid that he might be angry when she told him about how she could manipulate people.

"Yes. All mermaids are born with the power of persuasion, whether it be a physical or vocal power. We usually have a little bit of both, but one side is usually much more dominant than the other."

She took another breath before continuing.

"My strength is vocal. A human will usually do whatever I tell them to at that moment and will not even remember anything I said the next. Kat and Nitra both have more of the physical power. They will use their touch, gestures and body language to get the things they want.

Aden looked down with embarrassment, not wanting to meet her gaze. Slowly he began to speak.

"It all makes sense now."

Kailani hated that he thought this was a power she held over him as well. Quickly she added, "But for some unknown reason, none of our powers work very well on you."

She felt better once he looked up at her again. His curiosity was piqued and she continued to explain.

"You can remember things that the others can't. You can choose to ignore the things we've asked of you. I saw Nitra shove you off that bridge. She shouldn't have had to do that. If she told you to jump, like you said, you would have done it right then and there, without a second thought."

His steely gaze was focused on hers and he listened intently as she finished what she was saying.

"I am sure that rejection made her very angry," Kailani continued, "She is used to getting everything she wants. She's not used to being told no. Ever."

Kailani paused, not quite sure of how to continue now. Breaking eye contact, she looked down, then back up Aden's flawless, chiseled body, taking in every delicious inch of him. Even though his skin was a little paler and his clothes were still wet and slightly tattered, he still resembled complete perfection. He looked as if he were a model, straight off the pages of a magazine, coming from a recent photo shoot.

Finally she found her voice again.

"Honestly, Aden. I am so glad that you are alive, but I have no idea how you survived that fall. I was sure that you had broken your neck and drowned. Yet here you are, looking more than healthy, moving around as if nothing ever happened."

She was about to ask him how it was that he was able to do that, when Kat showed up with her potion and Aden's water. Her sister had even thought ahead, knowing she might need one of her skirts so she could slip into it before the transformation.

After a quick sip of the potion, Kailani had her legs back again. She saw the way her sister was looking at Aden and knew exactly what she was about to say, before she even said it. Kailani braced herself.

"I'm glad you're alright," Kat told him, rubbing his back. "And I really am sorry about what happened yesterday at dinner, you know, with your father."

Kailani gave her sister a pointed look, silently telling her that was quite enough.

"What?" Kat silently answered back, narrowing her eyes.

Without waiting for a response from her sister or Aden, Kat quickly turned back to the cottage and started to walk away.

Kailani could see the pain in Aden's eyes as he was suddenly reminded of the horrific events from the other evening. She knew her sister had meant well, she just wished that she had given him a little more time. Looking at him now, Kailani could see that the strength of his presence, the strength which she had always been so attracted to before, was now gone.

In its wake was a look of defeat and complete exhaustion.

She knew that everything had happened to him so quickly, in less than a forty-eight hour period. It had to be taking its toll. She knew that for anyone, it would be overwhelming.

Kailani rose to her knees, trying to be strong for him, pulling him up to join her. She wrapped her long, slender arms around his neck and held him in a comforting embrace.

He placed his arms around her waist then burrowed his face into her neck as if this might make everything else go away. He squeezed her tightly at first, but then she felt him relax into her. The pulsing sensations that were exchanged between the two of them were now calming and soothing and he continued to let her hold him like that for a long time.

Never before had Kailani felt such a flood of emotion and she knew that if it were at all possible, right now she would be crying.

"Come. You need to rest," she whispered in his ear before she tried to pull away, so that she could help him to his feet.

Her action was met with resistance as he pulled her back to him, his arms tightening around her.

"I don't want to leave," he said softly.

"You don't have to. You can stay here with us. We'll just go up to the cottage so you can lie down for a little while."

"I should probably call Alana, at least to tell her where I am. I'm sure she is worried."

"Don't worry about that. I'll get Kat to do it for you."

Aden released his grip around her waist, then moved slowly away, but only enough to bring his face close to hers. He kissed her gently on the lips, silently thanking her. Her heart ached for him. She pulled him up from his knees and they walked slowly together, up the beach and toward the cottage, hand in hand, through the late afternoon haze.

Chapter 12

Annessa

*A*nnessa picked up the golden strand of hair off the top of her crystal ball and the transparency of the object returned to its original, opaque pearl luster. This fragile pearl was safely nestled inside its giant aurous shell case, so she closed the lid and clicked it shut.

She'd been watching as her granddaughters rescued this strange boy, Aden, from her sadistic niece. She had been able to witness the entire event through Kailani's eyes using a strand of her golden hair that created the magical link.

The pearl had been a gift, passed down to her from her father, Victor, the former Sea King. It allowed her the ability to see anything she wished as long as she obtained a personal possession of the one whose visions she wished to follow.

Next to the pearl's giant gilded shell was an ornate silver chest filled with various objects belonging to a wide variety of her subjects from across the four corners of Annessa's undersea kingdom. Using their possessions, she was able to keep track of many of the warriors, guards and healers as well as the adolescent adventurers whom she'd sent to roam the dry land in search of the various information, plants and ingredients that she had requested.

When she saw Kailani kiss Aden on the beach that night after the dance, she had immediately called her home to the palace, to remind her of the dangers that she had been warned about when falling in love with a human.

Once she was back at the palace, Kailani had described to her all of the energy that seemed to emanate from around him and told her that Katiana and Liam had been able to feel it as well. It sounded very similar to a report that she had received long ago from several of her pet sea turtles. They said they had also felt a similar energy radiating off of a young boy, when they had ventured onto land one night, to lay their eggs. It happened to them around the same area, near the Tampa Bay, about a decade ago.

Annessa swished her silvery-purple tail, propelling herself to float over to the long amber window of her master suite, high up in the tower of the coral palace. It was the same palace that had once belonged to her father, the same palace that she had shared with all of her sisters, back in their youth, so many years ago. As the eldest, she had rightfully inherited his estate, along with all of the pleasant and painful memories.

A constant, peculiar blue radiance lit the grounds of her enchanted kingdom below. As she looked out the window, through the surrounding Atlantic Ocean, she ran a worried hand through her clipped ash-blond hair, which had recently become streaked with strands of silver. She had long ago gotten used to its shorter length, but still, every time she touched it she was reminded of her favorite little sister and the sacrifice that she had made to the sea witch, trying to save her life.

She opened up the amber window to let in some fresh water and looked down, past the oyster shell roof that glittered with pearls as the ocean's currents flowed through them, opening and closing the shells. In the courtyard below she could see the flower beds that she and her sisters had created as children. At the base of each of them, the sand glowed bright blue like flaming sulfur. The flowers that were planted inside them were a combined deep blue and bright red. They had blossoms that looked like the flames of a fire.

The flower garden Annessa had made was a vision of the night sky complete with the moon and stars. It was her favorite thing to see whenever she ventured up to the surface. Nearby she could see the shape of Vanessa's mermaid as well as Marissa's whale. They were right there alongside her other sisters' landscaped pieces of art.

In the far corner of the gardens was Calyssa's flaming red sun. Standing there beside it was a rose colored weeping willow with thick branches that now completely covered the white, marble statue below.

To someone just passing by, it looked like a normal tree, but inside it housed a secret that few knew was still there. The statue was of a human boy. Annessa's baby sister had found it one night after a terrible shipwreck and afterwards she seemed to be obsessed with it, along with the world above the sea.

She continued to think about Calyssa. She remembered how quiet and thoughtful she had been, yet gentle and loving at the same time. She could still visualize her stunning blue eyes, always so deep and soulful. Her clear rose-colored skin had always appeared to be so delicate. Annessa fondly remembered how kind her little sister always was to everyone, too kind sometimes. She was always putting others before herself. Anyone who ever met her couldn't help but to fall in love with her.

Calyssa had also been their father's favorite. His baby girl. Annessa remembered how devastated he had been when he heard the news of her death, how his heart had been broken to a million pieces. Calyssa had been the first of their kind to fall in love with a human and it hadn't worked out so well for her.

Annessa then thought about how her own daughter had also lost her life, because of her love for another human boy. She now worried that her granddaughter, Kailani, was following down the same dark path.

Even with these tremendous losses, Annessa knew that not all humans were bad. She had even made friends with one of them, many years ago, off the mountainous coast of Le Locle, Switzerland.

He told her that he was from Odense, Denmark and had grown up in Copenhagen. She recalled the name that he had given her that day. Hans, Hans Christian Andersen. He had then told her that he wasn't surprised at all to find out that mermaids really did exist. He explained that he had actually met a woman named Agnete, who'd told him from her personal experience all about the mermaids and their underwater world.

Hans and Annessa had spent many nights together on a secluded beach, getting to know each other and swapping stories. Her favorite was the one he had said inspired him as a child to become a writer. It was called Arabian Nights. She would then go home and share all of his wondrous stories with her sisters.

After Calyssa's death, Annessa told Hans all about her sad, tragic story and how her sister's irrational decisions had ultimately led to her demise. She even tried her best to describe to him the transparent beings that she had seen come and take her sister with them, into the air that morning, after she had jumped from the ship.

He told her that he had been working on a collection of children's fairy tales and asked if he could include Calyssa's story. Annessa agreed, but only if he promised to leave out their names. He said that he thought that would be best, of course, as no one would ever believe him if he were to tell them it was a true story. He promised Annessa that by immortalizing her in his story, even though her sister was no longer around, she would never be forgotten.

He had made good on his promise, even letting Annessa read his book once it was finished and the two of them remained good friends for many more years until Hans's health began to fail. After that he was no longer physically able to make the journey to the beach to come visit her and sadly, she never saw him again.

Annessa fingered the deep blue sapphire stone that she had encased in a pendant. It was hanging on a long, silver chain that she kept constantly around her neck. With it's powers she had worked for many years to try to create a potion that would return the immortality to the souls of her and her people, the Mer.

The Mer had originally been blessed to live in the sea for centuries before their souls finally journeyed to the glorious afterlife. But long ago, even before Annessa's birth, Poseidon, the god of the sea, had cursed them all to return to the sea upon their deaths, their bodies and souls quickly dissolving into sea foam soon after. As far as she knew, there was no one that had lived in that dark time, still alive today, who could tell her the reason behind the curse.

Even with all of her efforts, Annessa had so far only managed to design a potion that created a temporary human effect on an adolescent Mer. It became ineffective once the Mer reached the age of eighteen, becoming a mature adult. She was still trying to tweak the formula so that she could figure out how to extend the life of this potion. She was now quite sure that she was only missing one key ingredient. The problem was, she had no idea what that last ingredient was and therefore no idea where to even begin looking for it.

Annessa herself had never been able to walk upon the land or to have a personal human experience. She had only been able to see things that were on the land, beyond the shore lines, through the eyes of others. Sometimes she would just lie on the sandbars, basking in the moonlight, watching the nearby town lights flicker and the stars above twinkle, the same as she had on the very first night she went to the surface, dreaming of what it would be like to be a human. Her favorite *thing about being on the surface was listening to the nearby music, coming from the bars and hearing the church bells ring.*

In this way, she was a lot like Calyssa, but as the oldest, she had a much more dutiful idea of her responsibility to the kingdom.

Before she knew the age limitations of her potion, Annessa's daughter, Madison, had used it to go and live on the land with a human boy that she had fallen in love with. She'd met him one day while she was exploring the islands in Hawaii. They had married young, while Madison was only seventeen, and conceived their twin girls only a couple of months later.

Right before her due date, Madison celebrated her eighteenth birthday and was frantic when she learned that her potion had stopped working and she was no longer able to return to the land to be with her husband. They spent the next few days on a secluded beach, near their home in Maui, where he would come to visit her as often as he could.

Desperate to stay with her and be with his new daughters when they were born, he decided to try Madison's potion just to see if it would have the opposite effect on him, turning him into a merman. They discovered instead that the potion had a lethal effect on human beings. He instantly stopped breathing and died right there in the sand, with Madison beside him on the beach.

Madison then returned to the sea all alone, frightened and broken hearted. She knew that mermaids usually lay eggs, beautiful, shimmering eggs, after procreation. They did not give birth to their young live, as humans do. Now that she was trapped back inside her mermaid form, she knew that her body did not have the anatomy to survive the birth of the live baby girls that she could feel kicking around inside of her.

She found a local healer by the name of Maggie and convinced her to try to remove her babies by caesarean. However, because this had never happened before, in the Mer world, Maggie did not have the experience, nor the knowledge to do it properly and Madison unfortunately did not survive the ordeal.

Annessa remembered rushing through the Panama Canal to get to her daughter when she found out that she was in Maggie's home in the Mid-Pacific. Because it was so far away, she wasn't able to make it in time. She just wished that she could have at least seen her daughter one last time, even if it was just to say goodbye.

To this day, she still felt tremendous guilt over Madison's death and blamed herself for allowing her daughter to consume the potion so early, while it was still at such an experimental stage.

Her only consolation had been that because Madison had married a human before her death, she had obtained an immortal soul and her body had not dissolved into sea foam. Because of this, she was able to give her a proper burial, back at her home, near the palace. She laid her only child to rest in her sister's garden, at the foot of her rose-colored willow tree. Annessa hoped that one day she would be able to find a way to lift the curse that had been placed on the Mer, as that would enable her to reunite with her daughter one day, once again in the afterlife.

Luckily, both of her granddaughters had been born mermaids, so she had been able to return with them to the palace and raise them as her own. During that bleak, sorrowful time, after Madison's death, they had been the only thing that had brought sunshine into Annessa's life.

Just then, an angelfish swam in through the open window and up to the troubled Queen. She stroked its fins for a moment, absentmindedly, before grabbing a small handful of algae flakes from her dresser drawer. The fish ate them quickly, content and happy with the tasty treat. It then swam around her, rubbing up against her skin and tickling her neck with thanks before darting to the undulating plants that grew out of her coral walls.

After being calmed by her own laughter, she watched it playfully ducking and dodging through the aquatic vegetation, before finally heading back out through her window.

She recalled the stories that her own grandmother had told her as a child, tales of the fish above the water and how they would fly through the air, living in the trees, where they would sing sweetly. Because the young Mer now had access to the land, she had been able to learn so much more about the world above the surface. She now knew these strange fish that her grandmother had spoken of, were actually called birds.

Annessa's own granddaughters would come back to the palace every once in a while, telling her stories of the things they had learned from their foreign studies.

She missed them both terribly, but had requested that they stay away as much as possible, to enjoy their short time out of the sea for as long as they possibly could. She knew that it would not be too much longer before they had no choice but to return home to the palace for good. Then, they would all be together again, for the rest of their lives.

Staring with her violet eyes into a nearby mirror, Annessa straightened the coral shaped silver crown on the top of her head. A movement in the reflection caught her eye and she then saw her husband, Richard, as he silently entered the room behind her.

Richard was the King of the Atlantic now. Strong and ruggedly handsome, he was also the leader of their formidable warrior forces.

He placed his barbed, stingray spear and leatherback, turtle shell shield onto the floor beside the door, then swam quickly into Annessa's outstretched arms. Wrapping his arms around her, he held her tightly, pressing her to his chest, still covered in the armor that she had woven tightly for him using seaweed and kelp.

Pulling back, she looked up at him and ran her hand through his short salt and pepper hair before kissing him softly.

"I've missed you terribly," he told her, then moved his head down to gently kiss her neck.

"And I, you," she sighed, giving in to this short moment of pure bliss.

Coming back to reality she remembered why he had left in the first place.

"How did it go?"

Hesitantly, he pulled back to look at her, his eyes full of worry as he relayed the latest information.

"Well, we managed to hold them off again this time, but the attacks are becoming much more frequent and intense. We were able to capture a few prisoners, for questioning, but something is not quite right about them. When they answer us, it is only in short phrases, with monotonic voices and no emotion. Their responses are delayed, as if they are unable to think for themselves, like they are empty shells, whose answers are coming from somewhere else."

He shook his head in frustration.

"We still haven't been able to figure out who is sending them or even where they are coming from."

Annessa frowned at this troubling news.

"And what about the soldiers we sent to the Southern Ocean, down in the Antarctic, to check on Marissa?" she asked.

The sorrow in his eyes was the unspoken answer Annessa did not want to hear and she looked away before he even had a chance to speak.

"I'm sorry my dear, but they still haven't returned. There is no word from them."

Anxious with worry for her sister's safety, Annessa had tried to track the soldiers, watching through the eyes of the captain of the mission. *She'd followed them closely, using her magical pearl, but shortly after they passed the tip of South America, the screen had abruptly gone dark. Because they had sent several search parties to the Antarctic before and none of them had ever returned, she knew that something was wrong and assumed her vision was being clouded by some sort of dark, unidentifiable magic.*

She was pulled from her thoughts by Richard's next question.

"How are the girls?"

It took her a moment to process his words before she was able to answer. She thought about telling him of this strange boy Aden and how he had appeared to her before, in the pearl, how Kailani was now falling in love with him. However, with all of her husband's responsibilities, she didn't want to give him anything else to worry about.

"They're good," she said, forcing a smile, "I just checked in on them earlier."

"Well, I'm relieved to hear that. Now that I know all of my girls are safe, I think I'm going to go down to the kitchen and see if the chef will prepare me something to eat. I'm starving!"

He started to pull away and head for the door, but before he could Annessa pulled him back to her.

"I'm glad that you're back," she said, kissing him again.

He held her tightly in his muscular arms and she felt the tension of the day melt away.

"I love you," she said in a whisper.

"I love you, too."

Richard released her and slid his large hand down her arm, into her palm, where he squeezed it gently before releasing it.

"Go eat," she told him with a smile.

He turned to swim toward the door and was about to leave when he turned back to her.

"You seem as if you're a little stressed," he said, "Would you care to join me this evening for a romantic, moonlight swim?"

Escaping the kingdom and venturing to the surface at night was one of their favorite things to do and she couldn't think of anything else in the world right now that might make her feel better. It sure beat staying in her room, worrying about Kailani and Marissa the whole time.

She looked over at her strong, handsome husband, floating there in the doorway. This was so typical of Richard to know exactly what she needed, when she needed it.

"I would love that," she beamed.

Chapter 13

Endlessly

After having taken a week off to recover from my adventure with Nitra, as well as the pain of losing my father, my first day back at school was unbearable. I couldn't stand all of the pitiful looks and remorseful comments that I was getting from all of my classmates. The only thing I really wanted to do was go back home, just to get away from it all.

My only consolation and the one thing that gave me the strength to make it through the morning was knowing that I would be able to see Kailani again during lunch, which was now rapidly approaching. I didn't know what it was about her, but somehow, whenever she was around, everything suddenly seemed better. She was like a beacon of light in my recent world of darkness.

I was pleasantly surprised when my Calculus class ended and she met me at the door, asking if I wanted to go eat lunch somewhere more private, with her, Kat and Liam. She really didn't have to twist my arm. I was more than happy to get away from all the hustle and bustle in our high school cafeteria and at the moment, nothing sounded better to me.

I put my arm around Kailani as we strolled leisurely out the back door of the high school, occasionally leaning in to kiss her glowing hair that reminded me so much of the sunshine. I took a deep breath, breathing in the refreshing aroma of her coconut scented shampoo as I let myself feed off of her radiant energy.

Once at the campus picnic tables we sat down quietly, claiming the bench across from Liam and Kat, who appeared so preoccupied and lost in each other's embrace that they seemed not to even notice our arrival. However, now that I knew their abilities, I knew that couldn't possibly be true.

Kailani must have said something silently to her sister because Kat then stopped kissing Liam and suddenly turned toward us. I noticed a brief narrowing of her eyes as she looked at Kailani before she turned to me.

"Oh, hello!" she said in a high-pitched voice, the same voice girls use when they are trying too hard to be nice. "Sorry about that. I didn't realize you guys had made it here yet."

I knew that she was lying, but I didn't say anything. I watched as she then reached into her lunch bag and pulled out several sandwiches.

"I brought everyone one of my favorites, tuna salad. Hope you don't mind."

When I took the first bite of my sandwich, I quickly realized that it had a lot more tuna and a lot less salad. The strong, fishy taste was slightly overwhelming, but I somehow managed to finish mine politely.

After we had all finished eating, Kat pulled out a small, chocolate cake with vanilla icing. She then lit two candles that were molded in the shapes of the numbers one and eight. This was done with a pink, blinged out lighter that she had pulled from her blue jean pocket. She then turned to look at Liam and sang the most beautiful rendition of "Happy Birthday" that I had ever heard. The whole time she never took her eyes off his.

The song was soft and sweet, intimate even, with just a

touch of melancholy. I began to feel as if I were an intruder, looking in on a private moment.

"I didn't know that it was Liam's birthday today," I whispered, turning towards Kailani.

"Well, actually it's tomorrow," she said, "but today is the last day they will be able to celebrate it here at school, together."

Her words reminded me painfully of the potion's age limit. Kailani hadn't told me about this on the day that I was almost killed, in fact she had only mentioned it to me just yesterday. She said that the reason she waited to tell me was because I was already too overwhelmed with the other information I had learned.

Today I was still wrapping my brain around what this fact would mean for us and our future.

Kailani continued to speak, bringing me back to the present.

"As far as everyone here at school is concerned," she said, "today is Liam's last day. He will be leaving tomorrow to go help our grandmother with our move to Denmark, remember?"

She was probing me and I nodded, now understanding the truth behind the lie.

I looked over to Liam as his birthday song was ending and after giving Kat a quick thank you kiss, he turned towards me and started to speak.

"Don't worry, I won't be far," he said, letting me know that he'd also been listening to what Kailani had said. "I'll still be around. I just won't be able to come up onto the land anymore. Queen Annessa has requested that I stay in this area to help guard the waters here around the island. She wants me to help make sure that the princesses are safe. Unless they send someone else, their only guardian that will be here on the land, will now be Mr. Spencer."

"Mr. Spencer?" I looked at Liam, confused, wondering if he was referring to Mr. Spencer, Kailani's music teacher. "Is he a Mer too? Isn't he too...old?"

Amusement lit up the expression of Mr. Popularity.

"Actually, Logan is an Encantu," Liam answered, "which is like a porpoise/human hybrid. They are very similar to the Selkies, as far as being able to come and go in and out of the water as they please, throughout their entire lives. However, unlike a Selkie, which are undetectable in human form, Encantu, while they are in their trans-formative state, leave evidence behind of their true identity. Haven't you ever noticed how he always wears some kind of hat? If he were to ever take it off you would be able to see a large blowhole gaping on the top of his head. These blowholes help Encantu to breathe more freely on the land. They have very small air pipes."

I glanced over at Kailani, sitting there next to me, and wondered why she had never mentioned this before. Liam, seeming to pick up on my slight irritation, paused for a second before drawing the attention back to himself.

"Logan is one of the Queen's most trusted guards in her court. He was sent on this mission, along with me, to help keep an eye on both of her granddaughters."

Liam then went on to say how much he was going to miss it up here on the land, along with all of the wonderful people that he had met and all of the things that he'd come to appreciate about our ways of life.

"I want to go with you," Kat pouted, looking longingly at him with her sad, deep blue eyes.

"No, baby. You should stay."

She dropped her head, so he stroked her cheek with his fingers until they came to a rest just below her chin. He lifted her face up to look into his because he wanted her to really understand the words that he was saying.

"You only have about five more months left to enjoy your experience here. After that, we will be able to be together everyday for the rest of our lives. I want you to enjoy this time, while you still can."

"It won't be the same without you here," she said, only pouting slightly less. She leaned over to kiss him again.

I squeezed Kailani's hand under the picnic table, once again reminded that our time together was also quickly running out. However, ours, unlike theirs, wouldn't be a temporary separation. Ours would be much more permanent.

I looked over at her, taking in the perfect features of her pale, angelic face and any irritation that I had felt quickly disappeared. Her long, golden hair was glowing bright in the sunshine and it amazed me to know that she was just as beautiful on the inside as she was on the outside. I knew for a fact that I could never be this lucky again and might never find someone so wonderful. It pained me to know that one day we might never get to be together, like this, again.

When she looked over at me, she tried to put on a brave smile, but it was traced with sadness and I could tell that her thinking was the same as mine. I tried to think of something to say that would cheer her up.

"Will you come over to my house today, after school?"

I whispered into her ear, using that as an excuse to kiss her softly on the cheek.

She only paused for a second before giving me her seductive, breathless reply.

"You couldn't keep me away."

Later that evening, Kailani helped me to finish my homework. Afterward, as I was stretching out on the bed, she stepped out onto the balcony for just a moment to get some fresh air. When she reappeared in the doorway, she was holding my old guitar. I then realized that I must have left it out there the night before, when I was practicing.

"You never told me that you could play."

"Well, maybe just a little," I replied modestly, "I mainly just play for myself."

I felt my anxiety increasing as she looked at me pointedly for a moment.

"Will you play me something?" she asked with a sudden burst of excitement.

I tried to think of an excuse to get out of this unexpected request.

"I don't know, I..."

"Please!" she begged.

After taking one look at those big, blue, pleading, puppy dog eyes with a perfectly plumped pout, I knew there was no way that I could refuse her wishes. I sat up on the bed reluctantly, crossed my legs and placed my guitar slowly, gently into my lap, trying to delay the inevitable.

"Any requests?"

She shook her head no, prompting me to pick.

After a moment's contemplation, I decided to play her my

favorite Green River Ordinance song, "Endlessly." That one always made me think of her.

I strummed along the first few notes and it surprised me when, shortly afterwards, she knew the words and began to sing along.

With our eyes locked on each other, I continued to play, mesmerized by her voice, singing the words to the rhythm of the notes that I was playing. I found myself wishing the song would never end, so that she would never have to stop singing.

By the time she sung the last note and the music had come to an end, the air between us had become so magnetically charged, it felt like my entire body was tingling like a live wire. Never losing eye contact, she climbed up onto the bed and crawled toward me, pushing my guitar to the side.

Even though my legs were still crossed, she wrapped her arms and legs around me so that she could sit in my lap. This took me off guard. I thought she was going to kiss me, but at the last moment she pulled back teasingly.

"You were amazing. I've never heard anyone play that well before, not even professionally," she said before finally putting her lips on mine.

At first the kiss was soft and tender, but it quickly became more intense and passionate. As I kissed her back, I allowed myself to completely give in to the moment and I could vividly feel every sensation as it coursed through my body. This kiss felt so natural, so right.

Neither of us was able to consciously decide the next move we should make. We went along with the ebb and flow, feeding off each other's energy, completely lost in this powerful emotional attraction that we both felt.

Finally taking control, I lifted her off of me effortlessly as I continued our passionate kiss, while turning my body. I held her graceful neck in one hand as I lay her head down gently onto my pillow. I couldn't stop myself from then kissing her soft neck, enjoying the sounds of her pleased responses.

A sudden knock on the door immediately brought me back to reality.

"Aden," said a soft voice from the other side.

It was Alana.

We sat up quickly, grabbing the nearby books, pretending to be busy finishing our homework.

"Come in!"

Alana poked her head through the door.

"I just wanted to talk to you about something."

She glanced nervously over at Kailani.

"Is this a bad time?"

"No. You're fine," we both answered together.

Kailani stood and gathered her purse from the night stand. She was still a little flustered.

"Actually, I have to go anyway," she said. "I was just about to leave."

She turned back to give me a quick kiss on the cheek before heading out the door.

"See you tomorrow," she said with a wink.

Alana came over and sat down apprehensively on the bed beside me.

"It's about what your father said, that night at the Samhain dinner. 'Use Tiwaz,' remember?"

I nodded and she continued. "I know what Tiwaz is."

"You do?" I asked in wonder, my eyes getting bigger.

"Yes. It's an ancient rune. Tiwaz is the seventeenth rune of an ancient alphabet. It was named after the Norse god Tiw."

I looked at her and thought, what does this have to do with me?, but she just kept on.

"He was the god of battles and justice, the protector of warriors and a mariner of courage and compassion. He would be the Norse equivalent of Zeus, or Jupiter."

She paused for a second to let that information sink in.

"The symbol of the rune Tiwaz is a vertical line, with a broken horizontal at the top," she told me, then trying to draw the shape she was describing in the air with her finger. "It kind of looks like the shape of an arrow."

My hand instinctively reached for the moonstone around my neck and I pulled it out from underneath my T-shirt.

"Does it look like this?" I asked as I held it out to her.

She looked at it carefully.

"Yes. That's it! I had completely forgotten you had this. Now I remember seeing you wear it, that first day you moved here."

I wanted to tell her that I had also worn it every day since then, it had just been hidden underneath my t-shirts. After a second thought though that information just seemed irrelevant.

"But, I don't understand," I said instead. "How am I supposed to 'use' it?"

I looked down at the moonstone, turning it over in my fingers as if this might unlock some of its secrets.

"To evoke the power of a rune," Alana told me, "you must trace the lines of it with your finger, then speak its name aloud. Before you can do this, you must perform a ritual on the object that the rune has been carved into. This will allow it to charge the object, infusing it with its magical powers."

"Do you know how to perform the ritual?"

"Well, no," she said, sounding a little disappointed in herself. "I've never actually done it before, but I know Mom has a book that will show us exactly what to do."

She grabbed my hand, pulling me toward the door.

"Come. I will show you."

Chapter 14

Come Home

Alana insisted that the ritual be done on a Tuesday night, at precisely 9pm. She claimed that both of these details directly correlated to my particular rune. The days crawled by and over the past week I'd become really impatient and irritable waiting for this day to come. Now that we'd figured out exactly what needed to be done, it was like torture, knowing that I had to wait even longer to follow out my father's instructions.

On the positive side, it gave us plenty of time to gather the items that we would need and make sure that we had everything. It also gave us the chance to study the spell in the book and prepare ourselves accordingly with the knowledge that we would need to perform the ritual properly.

As I walked into Alana's bedroom that night, I was overwhelmed by the vast array of bright colors on the walls. How come I had never noticed them before? Maybe she had recently painted?

Every wall was covered in a different color. As if this visual stimulation weren't enough, she even had her vivid purple bedspread covered in overdoses of bright, jewel-toned throw pillows. On the ceiling, in the middle of her room, there was a glass bead chandelier that was lit up, bouncing prisms of rainbow colored lights all over the place. I felt like I was trapped inside a giant kaleidoscope.

Directly underneath the chandelier, Alana had set up a

small, round table that she had covered in a bright red cloth. The table itself was short and only sat about a foot off the ground. The red cloth had been perfectly measured to fit the table and had been cut to where it was barely touching the floor. On top of the table burned a stick of incense which was stuck into the groove of a wood burner, with stars etched along its length. As I inhaled the aroma, I recognized the scent of lemon, cinnamon and sandalwood, as well as a few other blended notes that I couldn't decipher.

I noticed she had not quite centered the burner on the table. I knew that spot had been reserved for the rune. About two inches from the edge of the table, there were seventeen red candles, placed in intervals, forming a perfect circle. Each candle was held upright by a simple clear base that gave the illusion they were floating. Alana sat there beside the table, cross-legged on the floor.

"It's almost time," she said, looking at the clock before looking up at me.

She extended her left hand with her palm facing up.

"Hand me the necklace."

I reached behind my neck to undo the clasp, then passed it to her. I was more than ready to get this thing started. She placed the necklace onto the center of the table, inside the circle of candles, making sure that the symbol etched on the moonstone was facing up before looking back at me.

"The ancient runes are powerful universal energies of creation. They reside in the Infinite Quantum Ocean, a mysterious place where time does not exist. Inside this place, there is no past, present or future, only the now. The rune's energies allow you to develop and master your own personal, spiritual and psychic powers. There are a total of twenty-four original runes, but the specific energy that we are calling on tonight is Tiwaz, the warriors' rune, energy of courage and justice."

The clock on the wall chimed to signal that the ninth hour had arrived.

"Turn off the lights," Alana told me in a hushed voice.

After doing so, I came back to the table and sat directly across from her on the floor. She closed her eyes and began to hum. After she opened them again, she lifted a small staff off the floor which was covered in carvings, images of the many different ancient runes. I recognized the familiar shape of Tiwaz amongst them.

"Tiwaz!" she bellowed in a voice so loud it startled me. "We call upon your power and ask that you evoke your magic into this moonstone."

She touched the necklace with the top of the staff and held it there for several seconds. She then gently placed the staff back down on the ground and sat up, beginning to trace the rune on top of the moonstone with her finger.

"Tiwaz," she now whispered, signaling for me to say it along with her.

We then repeated the name seventeen times. After the last, she looked over at me and nodded. Simultaneously we blew out all the candles.

After sitting there in the pitch blackness of her room, for what seemed like forever, I decided to break the silence.

"Did it work?"

She crawled over to the wall and turned the lights back on.

"I don't know."

She stared at me for a moment before we both decided to look down at the necklace. Even though the colorful lights from the chandelier were making the moonstone glow, it didn't appear any different than it had before the spell.

Alana grabbed the necklace off the table, gingerly holding the pendant.

"It is now what is called a bind rune. So, supposedly, in order for you to be able to evoke the power that is inside, all you need to do from now on is trace the rune with your fingertips, then speak its name aloud."

She used her finger to go over the etching, then closed her eyes, still touching the moonstone.

"Tiwaz," she said, focusing all of her concentration and energy toward it.

We sat there for a moment, yet nothing happened.

Alana sighed in frustration.

"I'm sorry, Aden. I don't know what else to do."

Taking a deep breath, I tried to hide my disappointment.

"It's all right," I made myself say aloud.

"I'm sure that we will figure it out," she tried to reassure me.

I reached over and grabbed the necklace from her outstretched hand and reattached it around my neck.

"I think I'm just gonna go to bed now," I told her. "I'm suddenly feeling really tired and drained."

She frowned at me, but apologized again.

I closed her bedroom door behind me and walked down the short hallway to my room. After making sure that my door was shut tight, I plopped down onto the bed and started staring up at my star covered ceiling, something that had become quite a comfort to me. It was then I began to feel the effects of how truly exhausted I really was. This had been my only lead in trying to figure out what my dad had meant by "Use Tiwaz." Now I'd have to start completely over, back at square one.

Frustration consumed my thoughts. Where was square one? I was so far away from square one that I couldn't even see it. Now that the spell hadn't worked on this rune, I had no clue where to even begin.

So many factors were causing me stress. As if the pressures of being a slightly normal, teenage boy were not enough, I now had to figure out how to "Use Tiwaz," something that up until a few moments ago I was absolutely sure was going to happen tonight.

On top of that I also had to help Kailani figure out a way to help her grandmother extend the age limit on her potion. If we couldn't succeed with this task, there would be no happy ending for us. This thought bothered me the most, for the one thing I knew for sure was that I couldn't even begin to imagine the rest of my life without her.

I decided to then say a prayer, asking the only God I'd ever known, my heavenly father, for his help and guidance. I told him my problems then decided to release them to him.

Immediately afterwards, I felt a renewed inner peace and was then able to relax. I knew the lonesome burden on my shoulders was no longer mine to bear alone. I knew that if there was a way, he would help me find it.

As I lay on my bed, drifting off to sleep, I traced the arrow on my necklace with my finger.

"Tiwaz," I whispered, barely coherent.

This time, as soon as I fell asleep, it literally felt as if I were falling. My entire body felt heavy, like it was dropping away from beneath me, and I rose slowly above my body, feeling like I was floating up, light as air. Looking down on my bed I was then able see myself. My eyes were closed, as I lay there asleep on the bed.

I'd never had an out of body experience before and I found this startling and completely terrifying. I continued to float up through the ceiling of my room, straight through the terracotta tile roof of the house. I climbed higher and higher through the night sky. As I looked down, the ground began to shrink.

A crippling fear began to overwhelm me as I realized that I didn't know how to stop myself and it dawned on me that I was no longer in control of the situation.

All of a sudden the glowing orbs of light from my earlier dream had returned. This time they floated closer and closer to me as we continued our ascent together.

"Come home," they called out to me in their ethereal voices. "Follow us."

Unsure of our destination I was hesitant, yet curiously, I somehow felt nostalgic as I regained some control of my mobility. I decided to follow their instructions.

I looked up to them, then left the world far behind.

When I glanced back down to the earth, it reminded me of looking at many of the pictures that I'd seen taken from the satellites in space. The blues and greens from the planet below were standing out in stark contrast to the blackness of the surrounding universe. Sporadic clouds created ever-changing patterns that covered the globe.

"We're almost there," the strange orbs called back to me. Their comforting voices were soft and delightful, and I realized that I was no longer afraid.

Chapter 15

Geode

At the end of our journey, we came to a stop on a rocky, barren landscape that glowed with a bright luminescence. After staring at it for a moment, I recognized that it was the moon's surface by the video clips I had seen in school. The ones that were documented by NASA on it's first lunar mission.

Pretending to be Neil Armstrong, I tested out the zero gravity thing by doing a few short, weightless bounces. Stellar!

I stretched out my hand in front of my face and realized that I could see straight through it. Strange, maybe I wasn't really here after all. I tried to touch it with my finger on the other hand and when it made the connection, I was surprised to find that it still felt solid.

Apart from my own breathing, the night was still, eerie and quiet. Looking around I noticed that all of the orbs that had accompanied me here on my journey had seemingly disappeared, with the exception of one. It caught my eye as it darted spasmodically around my feet.

"Down here," its soft, wispy voice called up to me.

I stared down at the glowing orb and there beside it I recognized the symbol of Tiwaz. It was etched into a large silver rock there near my foot. The orb of light fluttered around it like a moth near a flame.

I could almost hear my father's voice inside my head, "Use Tiwaz."

Remembering what Alana had taught me about how to evoke the stone's magic, I traced the rune with my finger then spoke its name aloud.

With the incantation, I immediately heard a grinding sound begin as the rock below slid away to reveal a secret passageway that was hidden underneath. The orb of light flew down into it and I quickly followed suit.

The passageway was a large, spiral stairway that was carved from the same type of stone that had been part of the moon's reflective surface. The orb's light illuminated each stair as it led us down into the dark shaft.

"We've been expecting you," the tiny voice called back, startling me as it fluttered ahead, continuing its quest of showing me the way.

Once at the end of the staircase, the light led me down a small, dark tunnel and I could see very faintly that there was a bright light up ahead of us, at the other end, that made my guide's light pale in comparison. As we got closer to the end of the tunnel, the orb of light ahead of me faded and I was able to make out the faint, translucent form of a small woman. She was flying through the air, using the wispy wings that protruded delicately from her back.

As we stepped out of the darkness together, into the vast light, we stepped onto a small platform that stood high above the stunning landscape. I looked out and took in the unbelievably beautiful view that surrounded me. It seemed as if we were on the inside of an enormous geode.

Large crystals covered every inch of the walls of the gigantic cavern. Millions of those same glowing orbs floated through the middle of the open air, causing light to bounce off the walls and illuminating the crystals, which sparkled brilliantly.

As my eyes grew more accustomed to the overwhelming brightness, I could tell that each one of the orbs before me also contained one of the same winged, translucent beings as my guide.

I glanced over to get a better look at her. I was now able to see even more of her delicate features. She had short, faint brown hair, which flipped out at the ends, and her pretty face featured a small angular nose with pouty lips. Everything about her was translucent, except for her clothing. Hugging her tiny curves was a thin, white dress that was gathered in the middle with an antique silver belt. The buckle of the belt consisted of a large black stone that was so dark, it gave the illusion that she had a giant hole gaping through the middle of her stomach.

She looked over at me with her pale green eyes and a flitting, ghostly smile.

"It's my pleasure to finally meet you. I'm Faelyn," she told me as her sheer, white dress gently floated up around her dainty legs.

"As the Queen of the lunar fairies, I am also your assigned personal guardian. While this may be your first time being able to see me, I, on the other hand, have known you all of your life. I've been watching over you ever since you were a baby. I am so happy to finally introduce myself and be able to say hello to you."

She reached out her tiny, faint hand, which was barely big enough to shake one of my fingers.

Confused, I couldn't think of anything to say at the

moment so I just pointed out my finger and touched her dainty hand.

"Um...Hello?" I finally managed.

Instantly, before I could think of something else to ask her, she started down yet another staircase.

"Follow me," she instructed.

These stairs hugged the right side wall of the cavernous opening and gradually descended to the ground level.

"There's someone else here who would like to see you," she called back to me.

I could hear the hushed whispers of the other fairies as they floated through the air, their voices jumbling together as they bounced in echoes off the domed walls.

Our descent seemed to take forever, but we finally reached the bottom of the luminescent stone steps. Faelyn led me down a thin path, through a thick crystal forest that was full of jeweled flowers and strange silver plants which appeared to be made from liquid metal.

"Where are we?" I called ahead to her.

"We are in Selenia, the Lunar Kingdom. We are not far from the Crystal Palace."

As she spoke the words aloud, the forest cleared and I could see the brilliant palace, lit up ahead, standing tall upon the hill.

"Faelyn?, are we . . . ?"

"Inside the moon?" she asked, as if reading my mind. "Yes. We are. Welcome home!"

"Home?" I asked, now in a state of even more confusion.

"Yes. This is the place that you were born," she said quite frankly as she floated through the transparent doors of the palace entrance. In almost the same breath she asked, "Would you care for something to eat?"

For some reason she seemed very excited by the idea of me eating their food. She pointed over to a large banquet table that had been set up on the side of the massive antechamber.

On top of the table there were many silver trays piled high with small pill-sized spheres that were organized and labeled according to their many different colors. I managed to read a few as we came closer. Prime Rib, Grouper, Watermelon, etc.

"No, thank you," I uttered.

Unsure of this so-called food, I hoped that my refusal wouldn't offend her. It didn't seem to have any affect as she flitted on ahead to grab some of the little pill-like spheres off the table.

"Then here, take a few of these Philly cheese steak sandwiches for later. I know that they are your favorite. Just make sure to be careful! Each one of those little capsules is like eating a whole foot long sub."

Her tiny size only allowed her to carry two of the dark green spheres at a time, so I shook my head no when she turned back to get more as she continued to speak.

"We don't get very many visitors here, as you can imagine, so we have found a way to magically preserve the food that we have prepared. You don't have to worry about missing out on the taste either. Each of them is coated with their appropriate flavor crystals so they come bursting to life as you put them in your mouth."

Between her warm smile and the pride in her voice, I couldn't refuse her hospitality, yet I couldn't make myself try one at this moment, so I quickly placed them into my pocket.

I was eager to learn more from this strange experience.

"Faelyn?" I asked her, "If I was born here, that means you might know my mother. Her name is Melissa."

"Of course I know your mother," Faelyn said as she drifted over to touch an ornate set of platinum double doors that magically glided open.

I was about to ask her another question when she elaborated.

"I know your mother very well. Melissa is just one of the names that she uses when she visits the Earth. In reality she goes by many names, Diana, Selene, Dae-Soon, as well as many others. Here, all of us know her as Artemis, great goddess of the Moon and Hunt."

Faelyn beckoned for me to come stand beside her. Physically I obeyed, yet my mind was still reeling. I began to feel nauseous, like I was losing control again.

As I came around to stand in front of the doors, I paused in wonder. I felt her calmly touch my elbow as she reached out for me to follow her inside.

The doors opened up into a grand, resplendent room. On the far side of the bright chamber, on top of a set of lightly colored marble steps, sat a large cushioned throne. It was embellished on the top with a large set of golden antlers, that were welded onto it. In the seat of the throne sat a lovely, innocent looking girl who appeared to be younger than I. Her skin was brightly luminous and her long, straight hair was a fair, silvery blonde. She sat there motionless, patiently watching our entrance.

I heard Faelyn clear her throat.

"Aden. May I introduce you to our leader, the great goddess Artemis herself. Your mother."

I looked over at Faelyn just to make sure that I'd heard her correctly. She was bowing to this girl. She then straightened and nodded at me before gesturing me forward, toward the steps of the throne.

The beautiful, silent girl stood regally from her seat, then she rushed down the steps excitedly to meet me.

My first thought was there was no way this could be right. It was impossible for her to be my mother. She looked way too young. But I noticed as she came closer, I was able to see her eyes much more clearly. They were the same silvery grey as mine. Mesmerized, I held her gaze. It was almost as if I were looking into a mirror, seeing myself reflected in her perfectly flawless features.

I stood there frozen in place, unable to make my feet move to close the small gap that was still between us. When she finally reached me, she grabbed my shoulders and awkwardly pulled me into a long, firm embrace. She was surprisingly strong for such a slight figure.

"Oh, my baby boy," she said. "How I have missed you!"

She continued to hold me, pressing the side of her face into my chest. I looked down at her silvery blonde hair and realized that I had just heard my mother's voice for the first time. It was strong, yet soft and comforting at the same time.

I had no idea what to say back to her.

Sensing my apprehension, she looked up at me with a distraught expression on her face.

"Please know that I never meant to hurt you by leaving you with your father. I believed then, and still do, that it was something that had to be done for your own protection and his."

Her voice cracked ever so slightly at the mention of my dad and she pulled back from me before continuing to explain herself.

"You see, I was given my powers long ago by my father, Zeus, in exchange for my vow of chastity. At the time of my oath I had every intention to obey his rule and remained pure for many thousands of years. Unfortunately, I underestimated just how powerful the force of love could be and when I met your father . . . Anyways, the point is that Zeus and all of the other gods can be angry, petty and very jealous at times. I was afraid that if any of them ever found out that I had broken my vow, they would try to seek vengeance by destroying those who I love the most, you and your father."

She reached her hand delicately toward my neck.

"I gave Brogan that necklace you are wearing as a type of protection. It has the unique ability to act as a type of cloak, shielding your powers from the eyes of the gods. Normally a child of one of the gods does not begin developing their powers until their eighteenth birthday. That is why I told your father to give it to you then. However, Faelyn tells me that you've already begun to show traces of these powers. The fact that you were able to travel here tonight, in your dreams, confirms to me that she is right."

"I thought that it was the necklace which allowed me to do this," I said hesitantly. At least I had finally managed to speak.

"No, my darling. It's the power that is inside of you. Eventually, as it becomes stronger, you will be able to access this ability on your own, but for now the necklace acts as a conductor of your energy. It is able to magnify the forces that are just now beginning within you. Your power, along with the rune's energy, is trapped beneath the protective cloak and it is reflecting back to you. I'm almost sure that is why you are beginning to see some of your powers developing early."

I stood there for a moment, taking in what she had just told me. She had said powers, plural not singular. I briefly wondered what other hidden powers that I might have. I looked back at her and found my voice again.

"I have so many questions for you. I can't even think to begin to ask them all now. You are so beautiful, but you seem so young. I don't understand how you could possibly be my mother."

She smiled like she had just taken that as a compliment before answering me.

"I may look young, but I am not. I stopped aging when I was fifteen, the day I took my vow. I have looked the exact same ever since. Even I am not completely sure how old I really am. When you have all of eternity to live, the time just drifts by and you lose track of it. I lost count of my true age a very, very long time ago."

I felt my throat tighten as I thought of the next thing that I had to tell her.

"My father. He's…"

"I already know, sweetheart," she said, pulling me to her and hugging me once again.

She then put her arms around my neck and stroked the back of my hair soothingly. She reached up on her toes and kissed away the tears that had begun to form in the corner of my eyes.

"As soon as the accident happened, I went to see my uncle Hades, god of the underworld, trying to bargain with him to return Brogan's soul to me, but he turned me down, along with my offer. He then refused to give me any other information that I had tried to pry from him."

Suddenly she held me at arm's length before looking at me sternly.

"Listen to me carefully. There is something strange going on beneath the sea. After Faelyn informed me of the Selkie's attempt to take your life, we did some investigating. What we found gives us reason to believe that it was a Mer, not a Selkie who had something to do with your father's death. Therefore, we are now aware of two different species that may have a reason to cause you harm. However, just what that reason may be, we are not yet sure."

She gestured to her left then said, "Darling, there is someone else here that I would like to introduce you to."

A small orb of light floated up beside Artemis. As her light dimmed, I could see that she too was a young girl, with deep blue eyes and pale, rose-colored skin.

"This, sweetheart, is Calyssa. She is one of my guardians. Before her untimely death, she was once a Mer."

"Hello Aden," she said to me with sad eyes.

My jaw dropped in surprise as I put two and two together and the realization suddenly hit me.

"You...you're 'The Little Mermaid,'" I stuttered with disbelief.

She nodded slowly, frowning at me.

I turned back to look at Faelyn, as my realizations continued.

"The lunar fairies are the spirits from the story, that took pity on her at the end, taking her with them. You're the 'Daughters of the Air.'"

"Yes," Faelyn confirmed to me, shaking her head proudly.

Calyssa finally began speaking to me.

"Aden, I know that you are already in love with my sister's granddaughter. Having been in a similar situation myself, I know that there is nothing we can say or do that will change your mind about her. However, I do beg of you to be extremely cautious at all times, especially until we figure out the details of exactly what happened to your father and why.

Calyssa was now frowning at me again.

"As I'm sure that you are aware, there has never been a relationship between a Mer and a human, in all of our history, that has ever worked out."

The edges of her mouth turned up slightly before she continued.

"With that being said, as a believer in true love, I promise that I will do everything in my power to help the two of you find a way to somehow be together, forever."

"Thank you," I told her, sincerely. I had been touched by the emotion in her voice.

"I truly am sorry to hear what happened to you, with your prince."

She took a tiny, deep breath before responding.

"He never really loved me. In hindsight I can see that now."

Concern then clouded her features when she saw my silent, empathetic look and she continued.

"Just from hearing your story, I know what you and Kailani have is real and I have always truly believed that when two people really love each other, they should always fight to find a way to be together, against all odds."

Her kind words gave me hope, and I looked over to see

my mother walking up the stairs, back to her throne. When she reached it, she grabbed at something from behind it and pulled out a silver bow with matching arrows.

"Remember when you survived that fall from the bridge?" she asked, as she returned with the items to me.

How could I forget?

"Yes," I answered.

"Because you have the power of the gods running through your veins, we believe that makes you an immortal, both body and soul. That means your body will slowly, naturally heal itself of any injuries. However, because you are also still part human, we can not even begin to guess what kind of chinks there may be in your 'armor.' Because of this, I want you to have this enchanted bow, to use for your own protection. It is very special because you can still use it under the water's surface and your shots will be just as accurate."

As she finished telling me this, she winked at me.

I had only begun to contemplate what she meant by that last statement, when she then lifted her gaze up high, as if she could see something around us that no one else in the room could.

"The sun will be rising soon. Your ability to travel places through your dreams is only possible by the moon's light. I do have one more warning to give you, though. Even once you gain full control of your powers, you must still wear your necklace at all times while you are dream traveling. It is the only thing that creates a barrier of protection for your body against the possession of evil spirits who might be looking for a host to take over, while you are away. You must never travel if you ever lose it, or if you've taken it off."

With the seriousness of her warning out of the way, a lighter air passed over her and she kissed me on the cheek. The gesture was heartfelt, yet still held a sense of urgency.

"Goodbye, my sweet boy. Now that you know how, come back and visit us anytime."

She traced the carving on my necklace with her finger and said "Tiwaz."

With the mention of its name, the engraving lit up and my own vision blurred. Instantly I felt as if I were falling asleep, almost going into a trance-like state as I felt myself being pulled backwards, back down toward the Earth.

Before I was pulled completely through the walls of the palace, I could still hear my mother's voice, her words were becoming more and more distant.

"Remember," she said, "whenever you are looking up at the moon, know that I am here. I will be looking down on you, loving you from afar."

The backward force became greater, pulling me faster and faster through the floating orbs, through the crystal walls lining the inside of the moon's surface, before finally propelling me through space, back toward my home on Earth.

Chapter 16
Awakening

As soon as I entered back into my body, it jolted awake. I touched my face as the sun's first rays peaked in through the open curtains. Holding my hands out in front of me, I found that they once again looked solid. Remembering the bow and arrows that my mother had given me I looked around, but they were nowhere in sight.

How was I supposed to know if last night was real? Maybe it was just some crazy dream.

I lay in bed, pondering this for a while. Everything about that place had been like a fantasy land, yet every detail had seemed so vivid, so real. I tried my best to remember every moment.

My alarm finally snapped me out of my daydream and I made my way to the bathroom to take a shower and begin getting ready for school. I caught my reflection in the mirror and turned to stare at it. Now that I knew what Tiwaz was and the powers that it held, I was mesmerized by the moonstone hanging around my neck.

I kept thinking about my mother. My undead, or gone, very real -- assuming that I wasn't just dreaming -- mother. Looking up at my face, I tried to keep the image of her fresh in my mind, while comparing my own features to hers. She was definitely there, as was my father.

Taking a deep breath I leaned back stretching, then placed my hands into the pockets of my jeans, the same jeans that I had fallen asleep wearing last night. Deep in the right corner pocket I felt two small, round objects. As I pulled them out, I recognized the familiar deep green color, remembering the Philly cheese steak sandwiches that Faelyn had given to me the night before from the buffet.

Holy Cow! Last night *was* real!

I held one up with my finger and thumb, rolling it around slowly, remembering what she had told me about them. It was small, tiny even, barely the size of the nail on my pinky finger. It reminded me of one of the liquid mints that you can get at the drug store, only it shimmered with a slight glow and was hard like a rock.

I heard my stomach begin to growl. Weighing my options, I decided that I should just try one. What the heck, it would be a lot easier than going downstairs to cook breakfast and it would save me a lot of time too.

As soon as I popped the little sphere into my mouth, I could taste all of the mouth-watering ingredients bursting to life. Onions, peppers, roast beef, freshly baked bread, all in one little capsule. Breathing deeply, I could even smell the delicious sandwich.

After I swallowed, it was the weirdest sensation. I could feel my stomach immediately expand and it felt very full, as if I had just eaten a large sub. This was so cool!

Not to mention convenient.

A loud belch escaped my throat and I could then taste the onions all over again. I laughed out loud at this bizarre experience as I went to brush my teeth. Now I wished that I had brought more of them back home with me. Next time, I thought to myself smiling.

"I knew you would like them." I heard a tiny, smug voice say suddenly, making me jump.

"Faelyn?" I asked, after recognizing her lilting tone.

"That's right," she replied slyly, appearing out of thin air, "By the way, I hid your bow in the back of your closet, in case you were wondering."

I couldn't believe that she was here now, speaking to me.

"So it was real, everything that happened last night. I wasn't dreaming. My mother really is Artemis, goddess of the Moon and I really am an immortal."

"Yes, she is and yes, you are, but about that last part. I forgot to tell you, I want to make sure that you know, you must be extremely careful whom you choose to trust with that information. If it ever got into the wrong hands, our cover would be blown and that could be very dangerous for you, even fatal."

"Fatal? I thought my mother said that I could not be killed."

"She did, but remember when she mentioned the chinks in your armor? One thing we do know for sure is that, while a normal human being cannot kill you, another immortal can. While the necklace shields your power from their eyes, the information is still able to reach their ears. You must only tell those whom you know you can trust to keep your secret."

I heard a sharp knock on the door. Alana's voice yelled to me from the other side.

"Who are you talking to in there?"

"No one," I lied quickly.

When I looked back at the spot Faelyn had been, just moments before, she had already disappeared.

"I was just about to get in the shower," I yelled back to Alana, turning the water on.

I pulled my shirt up, over my head and went to take off my jeans before an unnerving thought occurred to me that I might still have company. My eyes scanned around the room.

"Faelyn, you better not be watching this," I whispered to the empty air.

Chapter 17

Chez Bobby

I decided that I had to tell Kailani.

I didn't want there to be any secrets between us, especially now that I knew she loved me. My head was reeling, but my gut told me that I could trust her not to tell anyone, just as I hoped that she knew she could trust me with her secret.

With a little bit of help from Alana, I planned the perfect romantic evening for us. Giving Kailani my big news at the end of the night would be my grand finale.

After school was over, I borrowed the Civic from Alana and drove over to Kailani's cottage to pick her up for our date.

"What is going on with you?" she asked suspiciously as I held open the passenger door for her, "You've been acting strange all day."

"You'll see," I told her, trying to keep the sides of my mouth from turning up. I found that I was unable to hide my enthusiasm. "I have something really important to tell you, but I want to do it at the right time. Can you wait till later tonight?"

With a slight frown she nodded, sliding gracefully down into the seat. Once she was in I closed the door, then made my way back to the driver's side.

"Where are we going?" I heard her ask as soon as I opened my door.

"I can't tell you that either. It's a surprise," I replied coyly, slipping into my seat.

"Just give me a hint!" she begged, pouting her lip.

For a moment I contemplated doing exactly that. She was making this so hard for me. At last I shook my head "no."

Looking straight ahead she gave an exasperated sigh, finally giving up.

The drive to our destination took us only a few minutes before we pulled up to a brand new dock, located on the bay side of the island. At the end of the dock was a large, white houseboat that had been transformed into a floating restaurant. The name "Chez Bobby" was painted on the side of it in large red letters, emboldened by green.

The loose, cursive font made it look as if it were someone's personal signature, perhaps the owner's. The words were underlined with a long thin version of an Italian flag and floating within the middle of the white stripe of the center, "Authentic Italian Cuisine" was painted in standard black print.

Small, white lights framed the boat's name, as well as the sign that welcomed us at the entrance of the narrow loading dock. The inviting twinkle of the lights continued around the rails of the boat and up the stairs to another dining deck on the second level, which was open to the clear evening sky above. There was a bar set up in the middle of it and I could see around the perimeter that they had set up little, red umbrellas to cover each of the bistro style tables.

I parked the car, then went over to Kailani's side to let her out. Taking hold of her hand, I could see a bright smile now lighting her face as I pulled her up. Seeing her reaction, once she figured out where we would be spending our first real date, was so gratifying that I couldn't stop my smile from mimicking hers.

I offered my arm and she quickly accepted it. Holding on tightly to each other we walked arm in arm, across the gravel parking lot, down the dock, then giddily up the ramp, to board the boat.

"Benvenuto," our hostess greeted us in Italian. She followed up in English with a, "Welcome to Chez Bobby."

After confirming our reservation, she indicated with a quick gesture of her hand that we should follow her and she showed us to our table.

I could hear the string quartet playing softly before we even rounded the corner of the kitchen and Kailani and I followed the hostess around to the front of the boat, where they had dining tables that were set up on the perimeter of an open dance floor.

We were seated at the very best table, right in the bow of the boat.

"Why are we the only ones here?" Kailani asked me, "I thought this was one of the island's most popular restaurants."

"Well, that's because I've been able to save all of my allowance for the past few months," I told her with a smirk, "I thought this would be the perfect excuse to spend it. I was able to rent out the entire restaurant for just the two of us this evening."

Her face lit up and she smiled at me sweetly, clearly touched by my, over the top, romantic gesture.

It was unbelievable how beautiful she looked at this moment. So happy and carefree in the fading sunlight. Her glowing blond hair was undone, cascading down her back in full, loose waves. On one side, she'd pinned it back with a small, purple orchid.

"You shouldn't have," she said, but she was unable to stop smiling, making me realize that it had been worth every penny. She moved her chair closer to the table.

My forearms were propping me up, because subconsciously I was drawn to her and found myself leaning across the table. She grabbed my hands, using them as leverage to pull herself up, out of her seat, so she could lean over to give me a soft, lingering kiss.

Time seemed to stand still and the rest of the world just melted away.

Even after the kiss was over, that refreshing, tingling feeling remained on my lips and I stared, transfixed in my chair, unable to take my eyes off of her, or keep the goofy grin from remaining plastered across my face.

The way she looked back at me made her seem even more sexy, sitting there with her tanned shoulders peaking out from the top of her strapless maxi dress.

"I'd do anything for you," I heard myself say, making her smile once again.

Throughout the evening, we ate some of the best homemade pasta that I had ever tasted in my life, all the while sipping sparkling grape juice out of elegant wine glasses. We talked and laughed as we enjoyed our time together, while a pleasant breeze blew in from across the bay.

As we finished our dinner, we watched the last rays of the sun disappear on the horizon. She moved her chair over to my side of the table so that she could sit closer to me.

"So...are you gonna tell me now?" she prompted.

I could tell by her expression that the suspense was killing her, but I had to admit that I was kind of enjoying this.

"Actually," I said, standing up, using this part of my plan to change the subject, "I was kind of hoping that we could finally have our first dance together. You know, the one we missed out on at the homecoming dance."

I reached out my hand to her and she began to smile.

"I would love that," she said as she took my hand. She now looked more excited than disappointed that I still hadn't shared my secret with her.

I pulled her to me and she threaded her arm through mine as I led her to the middle of the empty space they had cleared on the deck. More of the twinkling white lights were strung up above us, throughout the air, over the dance floor where they created a whimsical canopy.

I held Kailani tightly as we slowly swayed to the soft melody that was played by the talented quartet. Neither of us ever wanted to let go.

So far this had been the perfect date.

"This is the best night of my life," she whispered into my ear as if reading my mind. Her words sent chills down my entire body.

"I wish that it never had to end," I said.

She put her head on my shoulder and I looked up at the full moon, which had recently risen in the darkening sky. I closed my eyes and said a quick prayer, mentally preparing myself for what I planned to do next.

The realization of my mother's words and what they could possibly mean had given me a burst of inspiration and a plan had formed in my mind, consuming me with its promising possibility.

Of course, I also knew that there was a slight chance this

plan could get me killed. However, with the possible reward being so much greater than the risk, it was a chance that I was all too eager to take.

After our dancing, our sunset cruise was complete and the boat made its way back to the dock. After giving my thanks to the staff, I helped Kailani off the boat and back into the car.

Drawing in a few slow breaths, I tried to calm myself, but now that the time had come, I was starting to get extremely nervous. I placed my hands on the steering wheel, gripping it tightly to keep them from shaking. After a few moments I began to drive Kailani back to her home.

"You've gotten very quiet all of a sudden. Is everything okay?" she asked.

I smiled, looking over to reassure her that it was.

"Kaili, I had the best time with you tonight. It was more perfect than I could ever have imagined. I was thinking about how we never want it to end and I was hoping that now you would want to take a walk with me on the beach,"

I said this as we pulled into her driveway.

"Of course," she answered, rubbing my arm as she leaned into me. "Anything you ask."

After removing our shoes and leaving them on the closest dunes, we strolled hand in hand down the moonlit sand. Our journey was blissful and slow-going. We stopped every once in a while to embrace each other, sharing a few rapturous kisses.

"So..." she brushed my hair out of my eyes with her soft, gentle hand, "Are you gonna tell me now, whatever it is you've been keeping from me?"

I melted with her into the sand and held her tightly. I

kissed her softly on the forehead, this time I could feel myself trembling.

"I'd rather show you."

We sat on the beach and I looked up at the moon, silently saying a prayer. She followed my gaze to see exactly what it was that I was trying to show her. Taking a deep breath, I reached behind her and quietly grabbed the sports bottle she always carried around with her. I quickly untwisted the top, spilling a little in the process. As fast as I could, I took a large gulp.

Almost immediately, I felt my lungs collapse as they shriveled in my chest. I dropped the bottle, feeling the weight of it fall from my hand, as I began gasping for air.

Kailani looked back to see what was happening and her eyes dropped to my hands on my throat. I saw her eyes widen as she tried to figure out what exactly was going on. She reached for me and I could see the panic mounting in her expression as she watched me struggling for breath.

When her eyes finally caught the empty sports bottle lying on the ground beside me, she figured it out then started to scream.

"No!!! What have you done!? Someone please help! Kat! Liam!"

She closed her eyes, trying to telepathically summon her sister.

I felt as if I were sinking into the sand and couldn't draw another breath. I was quickly running out of oxygen. Slowly I began to realize that I had made a huge mistake.

I had been told that the potion kills humans and technically I was still part human. Then, another even more frightening thought came into mind.

While it may have been true that a mortal weapon could not kill me, this potion wasn't exactly made by a mere mortal.

With no oxygen left, I didn't have the breath to speak, but before I was gone I wanted to make sure that Kailani knew how much I loved her. I looked up into her crestfallen eyes and managed to mouth those heartfelt words to her.

I wanted to also tell her that I was sorry for this, but before I could muster up the energy a familiar blackness closed in all around me and I felt myself lose consciousness.

Chapter 18

The Promise

The coolness of the water splashing all around me, as well as the gentle lull of the surrounding waves roused me awake.

I could feel Kailani there beside me before I even had a chance to open my eyes. She was cradling me in the dark water, holding me with one arm behind my knees and one arm behind my neck, to keep my face above the water.

This was only the second time that I had awoken with her there beside me, but already I wished blissfully that it could be like this every time. My eyelids fluttered open and my gaze quickly settled on her soft, angelic face, lit by the moonlight. She dropped my knees, giving me a relieved smile. She then began stroking my face before she kissed me tenderly.

"You're awake."

Her energy flowed through me, causing my heart to beat faster. I realized that the air around me felt heavy, as if my chest had somehow been compressed. Instinctively, I tried to take a deep breath, but it felt as if my lungs were not working properly.

The funny thing was, I no longer felt the need to keep gasping for air.

Feeling a slight tickle behind my ear, I reached up with my left hand to scratch it. Instead of my normally smooth skin, I felt a couple of large slits that were alternating between being open, then closed, as they forced the water to flow through them.

I couldn't believe it. I had gills. Like a fish!

My plan had worked. I had been right! I'd convinced myself that the potion would have the opposite effect it did on the Mer, when it was consumed by a human. I also correctly guessed that because of their fragile structure, that was why a normal human being was incapable of surviving such a transformation.

Straightening out in the shallow water, I floated on my back, using the light of the moon to catch a glimpse of my newly formed tail. It was a deep, gray color. It was long and muscular, and the sandpaper texture of it reminded me of a shark's skin. Concentrating, I tried to move it. Stunned, as well as pleased, when it thrashed powerfully from side to side. I felt myself being propelled backwards through the water.

Fascinated, I reached out to touch it and noticed that I now also had a transparent web of skin that connected all of the fingers on my hand. I was grinning from ear to ear, pleased at myself because my theory had actually worked.

I looked up at Kailani, who had swam over to meet me. When I saw her expression, it was not one of delight, as I had expected.

Instead, she looked extremely vexed.

"Surprise!" I said sheepishly, trying to lighten the mood.

The angry way she was staring at me made it impossible for me to maintain eye contact.

"I thought you were dead!" she yelled at me, slapping my arm, "Right after your little stunt, when you stopped breathing, there was a few long, agonizing minutes before your transformation was complete. I had no idea that you were even still alive until I saw your gills begin to develop. Before that happened, I just kept screaming my thoughts for Kat to come and help us somehow, not that there would have been anything she could have done! She got here just after I saw your gills manifest and she helped me move you into the water."

As she spoke, her words gradually became less and less heated. Finally she took a deep breath, continuing her thoughts.

"When we are in Mer form, our lungs allow us to breathe outside of the water, but it is very limited and feels a lot like breathing through a pillow. The valve that protects our lungs is then much thicker. It is designed to keep the water out as we dive deeper."

I accepted this information, but my confusion must have been clear to her in my vacant expression.

"But I'm not like you," I said. "This tail is nothing like the ones I saw on you, not even Nitra. It's not shiny, nor beautiful."

Kailani rolled her eyes, clearly still agitated with me for my previous actions.

"It's a merman's tail," she said, "All of the men in our species have them. They are built more for strength and speed than our own. The female tails are more flashy. They are designed to attract and allure."

She paused for a second, as if she had just remembered something and I saw suspicion suddenly overtake her riled, yet still seductive features.

"Enough of that," she said abruptly, "What I want to know is exactly how did you survive that transformation? No human has ever been able to do that before."

Now was my moment. This had been the whole reason for my little trick.

"Well…that's because I'm not exactly human." I answered tentatively, with a sly smile.

At first she gave me a look, as if she thought I were joking, but after realizing that I was dead serious, all of the agitation left her face and she began to listen in wonder as I told her all about what had happened to me the previous night.

I started with the dream traveling to the moon, then told her about meeting Faelyn, my mother, even Calyssa. When I mentioned Calyssa's name and confirmed her identity, Kailani's mouth dropped open, surprised to find out where her great-aunt had been for so long and that she was actually still alive.

Kailani even appeared a bit emotional when I told her that her grandmother's youngest sister had even promised to help us in whatever way she could. I thought for a second that she was about to cry, but then I remembered she had told me before that this was an impossible task for her kind.

I warned her of the dangers Faelyn mentioned of revealing my immortality secret and she promised me that she would never tell anyone, not even her own sister. I then promised her in turn that I would never reveal her secret to anyone as well.

I felt as if a weight had been lifted off of my shoulders and we existed in a moment of complete honesty, comfort and trust in each other.

"My potion should be wearing off soon," she said, hugging me close to her, "If you'd like, I can take you for a swim, under the water. Let you see a little piece of my world."

I felt myself begin to smile and my head immediately began

bobbing yes. I took her hand firmly in mine, excited to begin this part of our adventure together.

"Our world," I corrected her.

No sooner had I finished speaking those words, her legs fused together and returned to the glorious tail I remembered from that first day, when I had found out about her true idenity on the beach. Somehow tonight her scales looked even more beautiful as they flashed first lavender, then turquoise, in the bright moonlight.

Releasing my hand, she slipped her purple maxi dress up over her head and tossed it up on the beach beside the outfit that I had been wearing earlier. She was wearing a shimmering turquoise bikini top that matched the color of her tail perfectly.

I caught myself staring and shook my head to clear my thoughts, taking in, with wide eyes, this masterpiece of art. I then recalled a story that she'd shared with me a few days before.

She had told me that when the adolescent Mer were able to walk upon the land, they had also been given the responsibility to collect and bring back as many bathing suit tops as they could, to share them with their people. They had quickly figured out the humans definitely had gotten this item of clothing right. These tops were infinitely more comfortable than anything the Mer were able to manufacture, limited as they were to using items found in or around the sea.

"Let's go!" I exclaimed, now that she was ready.

No longer able to control my excitement, I dived rapidly below the waves.

Getting used to my tail was easy. When I moved it left, my body went right. When I moved it right, my body went left.

After a few quick swishes it began to feel so natural, as if it were just an extension of me. I felt as if somehow it had always been there, hidden deep down inside of me.

I felt free at last!

The deeper we swam, the quieter everything around us became. I glided effortlessly through the dark blue waters, enjoying the peacefulness and serenity. Before tonight, whenever I would go swimming in the ocean, the water had always seemed cloudy. Now, everything around me appeared so clear. It seemed as if I were wearing a mask that was equipped with night vision goggles.

As my confidence grew, I began to swim even faster and faster, deeper and deeper. After a while, as I was reveling in my new found form and abilities, I noticed a quick flash of grey on my right side, turning just in time to see a bottle nosed dolphin as it raced up beside me.

Turning back to where I thought Kailani was, there on the left side, beside me, I became aware of the fact that she had fallen a good ways behind. I heard her making a series of loud, chattering noises that echoed through the water. To my surprise the dolphin then answered her back in his own wordless chatter. I couldn't understand what it was that they were saying to one another because I had not yet learned their language, but I was determined then, that one day I would.

I reached out to pet the dolphin on his head, as he was still there beside me. I was delighted when he met me half way with his nose, gently nuzzling my hand. I could feel the playfulness that was radiating from inside him and I had to admit that it was contagious.

Kailani swam up beside me and I felt her place her hand

on my arm. Inside my head I could now hear her voice. I was shocked to find that it sounded so much clearer than anything I'd ever heard her speak on the land.

As I looked at her face I noticed that her lips had not moved, yet I had undoubtedly heard her say, "He wants to race you."

Instinctively I started to say something like normal, but nothing came out of my mouth except a bunch of bubbles. Grabbing her forearm, I tried to communicate back to her by concentrating on the words that were forming inside my head.

When I heard her answer, "Yes, I can hear you," I knew that it had worked.

Pleased with this progress, I relayed a longer thought to her.

"Tell the dolphin that we can race each other around the island if he wants. The first one that makes it back here, to you, wins."

She gave him my message with more of those strange, audible chirps and then she turned back to me, smiling gleefully.

"On the count of three," I heard her say, before releasing my arm.

I watched her swim up ahead and pull a long piece of seaweed out of the sand, laying it down flat in a straight line. She turned back to face us and made another chirping noise, as I saw her hold up the first of her fingers.

Mentally preparing myself for the race, I watched as she held up a second finger. As soon as she counted to three, I lurched forward, as did the dolphin.

I swam through the shadowy water as fast as I could, all the while wondering if I would actually be able to beat the much more experienced dolphin. I rocketed through schools of tiny fish and dodged sporadic clusters of floating seaweed.

I sped past grouper, snapper and even accidentally brushed against a bewildered barracuda.

Looking left, then right for my competition, I couldn't see the dolphin anywhere near me, so I began to slow down to take a look around. There was no way that I could have missed him pass me, so I knew he couldn't be up ahead.

No sooner had this thought crossed my mind, the sneaky porpoise shot right past me. He had been hiding directly behind me so that I couldn't see him in my peripheral vision.

"Oh, no you don't," I thought to myself as I quickly picked up my speed again.

Finally, I could see Kailani. She was waving at us, up ahead in the distance.

I had to admit that the dolphin was a fierce competitor, but right before we both reached the finish line, I felt a new surge of power come from deep within me and I blasted right past him, leaving him behind in my bubbles.

When I passed Kailani, I reached out my arm and hooked her around the waist, pulling her with me, trying to use her weight to slow myself down. However, I kind of underestimated the power I had and the momentum was just too much. It took us both down as we tumbled through the water head over fins.

When we finally slowed to a standstill, I was able to gather my thoughts. Still touching her waist, I was able to ask her if she was all right.

"I'm fine," she giggled, elated by the thrill of the ride, "Great job! You won!"

The dolphin swam up beside us, giving me the evil eye.

After a few loud chatters to Kailani, he quickly swam away.

I couldn't understand what exactly he was saying, but I could tell by his tone that he was being a sore loser.

Kailani turned to me, trying to keep a straight face.

"What did he say?" I asked her.

Bursting into laughter, she then managed to reply, "You don't even want to know."

After all of the excitement was over, we swam leisurely through the cool waters, hand in hand. Kailani explained to me that since the Mer could only speak to one another when they were physically touching, they had to rely on a sonic language to communicate with each other from a distance. Each word had a specific sounding bleep.

She said that they had also developed the ability to use these sounds to judge how far an object was ahead of them, just by bouncing their voices off it. Even though the Mer could see clearly in extremely low light, this echolocation ability came in handy whenever they were swimming in the blackest abyss, of the deepest parts of the vast oceans.

As we continued to talk, we swam further out from the island. Slowly I began to notice the temperature of the water, as well as Kailani's hand, beginning to drop, the deeper we went into the ocean. It wasn't long before the chill of them both caused my teeth to start chattering.

Kailani looked over at me with a frown.

"I'm so sorry. I completely forgot that your blood is still warm."

Quickly, she began swimming upward, dragging me with her toward the surface. As we ascended, she explained her comment a little more in depth.

"I actually discovered this earlier, while you were still unconscious. It seemed strange to me at first, but the more I thought about it, it makes perfect sense. When the Mer go through our human transformation, our blood remains cold. So why wouldn't the opposite be true for you? It's not that big of a deal. It just means that your body will go through its energy supply a lot quicker in its effort to keep itself warm. You will need to eat a lot more often than we do and you will never, ever be able to travel to the Arctic or Southern Oceans where the waters are constantly freezing.

"You can go there?!" I asked her in wide-eyed amazement.

"Yes, of course. A mermaid's blood is cold, which allows us to adapt to any surrounding temperature. Once we reach the freezing point, our blood has a special protein in it that acts as antifreeze to keep us from freezing to death. We then move at a significantly slower rate, but at least we are still alive."

This was so cool! I loved hearing more about Kailani and the fascinating world that she was from.

I could now see the faintest hint of a small circle of white light, way above our heads. The closer we got to the surface, the larger the light became. When we burst through the tops of the calm waves, I could clearly see the outline of the full moon as it gently bathed us in its basking glow.

Instantly I felt myself become warmer, then stronger, as if the powers deep inside of me were being recharged. Looking down at my neck I could see my mother's necklace hanging there. It was glowing just as brightly as it had the night Kailani and I shared our first kiss.

Still holding her hand, I pulled Kailani up against me,

kissing her passionately with that rapturous memory still in my mind. Our tails swirled around in a circular motion as we used them to keep our heads above the surface of the tranquil water.

After living in a brief moment of the pure happiness of our kiss, another thought popped into my head. I pulled back from her, ever so slightly.

"I'm assuming that this potion will only work for me until I'm eighteen as well?"

Taking a deep breath she sighed, then lay flat on her back, floating as she looked up at the moon. Linking my arm with hers, I leaned back in the opposite direction, so we could keep our heads close together. After a few thoughtful seconds she finally answered my question.

"I'm afraid that you're probably right. This has not completely solved our problem. It has just given us a few more months to be together. Instead of March, when I am no longer able to become a human, we now have until July, when you will no longer be able to be part of this world."

I looked over at her as she lay there, looking up at the moon, her golden hair floating weightlessly all around her. Illuminated in the bright moonlight, she looked even more beautiful than I ever remembered.

She remained focused on the moon as her perfect lips began to speak.

"Do you think that we are just being young and naive, thinking that things will work out for us, just because we are in love?"

Hearing the despair in her voice made me sad. I couldn't begin to think for a second that things might not work out for us. Now that I had found her, my life felt complete, as if I had finally found my purpose. After the loss of my father, just thinking about the rest of my long, eternal life, without her being a part of it gave me a physical pain, deep down inside my chest.

Raising my head out of the water, I pulled her upright to face me and stared directly into her large, loving eyes as I spoke to her, firmly yet tenderly.

"I promise you Kailani, I will never give up, no matter what. I will do anything and everything in my power for us to find a way to be together, not just now, but forever."

She smiled with my reassurance as she entwined her fingers with mine and drew me in to her for another kiss. I couldn't tell if the power surge that I felt was coming from her, the moon, or the water. Perhaps it was a combination of all three.

All I knew was tonight I felt invincible, as if I could do anything. I felt something rise up inside me, like the mystic tides that surrounded us, and I knew deep down in my heart that I had spoken the truth.

I knew that one day I would be able to make good on my promise.

Epilogue

*I*n the depths of the Pacific Ocean, deep inside the walls of the Mariana Trench, at the heart of the Pacific Kingdom, Queen Vanessa was able to monitor everything her oldest sister Annessa had been watching with her magical pearl. What her benevolent sister had failed to realize was that her pearl had a twin and everything one showed, so did the other.

On one tempestuous day, several months earlier, Vanessa's older half-brother Adrian had shown up at her palace asking for her help. He had brought with him this twin pearl, as a sort of thank you gift. Before that turbulent day, she had never even known she had a brother. Over the years, she had always wondered why she looked so different from her mother and the rest of her fair sisters. Adrian, however, had the same dark, lustrous hair and striking black eyes as she.

As it turned out, Vanessa discovered that her father, Victor, the previous Sea King, had once been involved in a love affair with Trina, the infamous siren, also known as the widely feared sea witch herself.

Trina had been Vanessa's true mother, yet Adrian told her that growing up he had always believed himself to be Trina's only child. He had only recently discovered the truth, long after his mother's death, when he returned to his childhood home and found her hidden diary.

In it, Trina had written about a daughter that she conceived by seducing Victor. Unfortunately, her daughter had been taken away from her by force, as soon as she hatched from her egg.

Trina, devastated yet undeterred, plotted her revenge as she continued to make big plans for her daughter's future. She left explicit instructions as to what she wished for her to do in her absence, if anything were to happen to her. Adrian, having been far too young at the time to remember anything that happened, told Vanessa as soon as he read the diary, it wasn't hard for him to figure out which of the Sea King's daughters his mother had been writing about.

Her brother told her of the abilities his special gift, the pearl, held. However, what he forgot to mention, at the time, was its twin. Vanessa made the mistake of testing it out when she used it to follow the vision of her daughter, Nitra. It was the same night she found Aden on that rocky beach, in Alaska.

Adrian remembered to tell her about the pearl's twin the following day, even showing her how she could use a dark spell, from their mother's book -- which had been a second gift he had given her -- to create a sort of cloak between the two. This meant that Vanessa could view the things she wished privately.

Vanessa never used her pearl again, without this cloak, for fear that Annessa might figure out someone had a way to spy on all of her affairs.

During the time Vanessa spent with her brother, Adrian had talked to her about his early childhood and how he had grown up in a cave, with their mother. He told her throughout the years, he had studied witchcraft, potion-making and spells, alongside her. Vanessa had always before felt a bit of resentment for the witch, feeling she had caused the death of her sister, but Adrian assured her that Trina was not evil. She had only given Calyssa what she'd asked for, the thing that she dreamed of most. After her death, out of his anger and despair, her father had killed Trina for it.

Adrian told Vanessa that the spell book, as well as the pearl, had been two of their mother's most prized possessions and he made her promise that she would guard them well. During his visit, he taught

Vanessa some of the things that he had learned from their mother. He showed her, in the book, the spells that he was unable to cast, as a male, because he lacked the tremendous power of a true, female, siren.

He also taught her how to extract the immortal soul of a dying human, encasing it in an enchanted entrapment sphere. By doing this, she was able to capture it, before it moved on to the after life. It had taken her several practice sessions to master this delicately evil craft, but finally she had it.

Adrian had also shown her how to preserve the empty shell of the human body that was left behind, transforming it into a Mer that could be controlled by its maker.

Using these tactics, the two of them had drowned hundreds of sailors and fishermen. They now had countless mindless, brutal warriors for their growing army.

As much as Vanessa had enjoyed Adrian's company, there were times when she wondered if he were somehow using her. She couldn't shake this feeling in the pit of her stomach that perhaps, he had his own hidden agenda. She guessed that there was some other reason for his reaching out to her, coming to her palace.

Because of this unwavering feeling, she knew she could never fully trust him.

After he left, she continued to practice, using the book. She now knew the formula to make the draught that had killed her youngest sister. For a price, she would now give it to any Mer that wished to become a human permanently.

The only problem with this draught was its stipulations. The Mer that drank it would be in constant pain every time they stood on their new found feet. Even if this pain was too much to bear, they would be stuck forever in their new human form. The only way to turn back was to kill the one they loved the most.

Her sister, Calyssa, had found this out the hard way.

There was no way to guarantee that the object of their desire would love them back. If they ever fell in love and married another, then the Mer would die the next morning. Their extended lives would be cut short, prematurely.

Vanessa knew, even though she wanted the ability to walk on the land one day, this draught would never work for her. There was no possible way that she could ever fall in love with a disgusting, repulsive human. She thought about how she had watched Kailani and Aden's relationship blossom over the past few months. Even now it still made her sick to her stomach.

Humans were vile, nasty creatures that polluted the oceans and waterways with all of their unnecessary wastefulness. They were so consumed with themselves, they had complete disregard for any other species. They arrogantly believed that they were the most intelligent, hence important, beings on the planet, so this meant they felt that they could do whatever they pleased to all of the others.

If they were ever to find out that the Mer really did exist, they would find a way to hunt them down, imprisoning them for their own viewing pleasure. Most of her kind would then be sacrificed, simply for their scientific research and experimentations.

Vanessa thought about how wonderful things had once been. Many years ago the Mer had been plentiful, thriving in the depths of the earth's oceans, coexisting peacefully. As it was now, most of them had been killed, including her first husband, along with several of their children.

The humans had done this.

Vanessa felt that the humans could have cared less about all of the lives of the creatures they destroyed. Not only had they killed her family, but countless whales, dolphins and other innocent animals had suffered the same callous and unnecessary fate that day.

She hoped they never discovered the truth. She wanted them to continue to ignorantly believe that the Mer only existed in their stupid, fabricated fairy tales.

Anger boiled the cold blood that was inside of her. Constantly consumed by an overwhelming desire for revenge, Vanessa knew the thing she wanted the most was to destroy them...destroy them all.

With the power of the god Hephaestus, contained in a ruby that she kept tightly fastened to an ornate golden bracelet, which decorated her wrist, Vanessa had the ability to cast pillars of fire at will. She could also create volcanic eruptions. With these powers alone, she had been able to kill a few humans at a time. As good as it felt, this had not been enough. This was not the fate they deserved.

She knew that if she could reunite all of the stones, controlling all of the elements at once, she would be able to create massive fire and ice storms, as well as epic earthquakes, tornadoes and hurricanes on a scale that the world had never seen.

She could use these mega storms to destroy every human being that was on the face of the earth.

With the Mer safely under water, they would then be able to repopulate the oceans, free of worry from above. Holding all of the power, she would then be the Queen of all the lands and seas on Earth.

Unfortunately, Vanessa also knew that most of her sisters were much more tolerant of these horrific humans. That being said, if her sisters ever discovered her plan, they would never allow it to happen.

It was with these thoughts in mind, Vanessa had justified creating the army. She wanted to use these brutal, compliant warriors to forcibly take over each of her sister's underwater kingdoms. She knew that this had to be done, before she would be able to gain possession of the mighty stones that each of her sisters were guarding. Her ultimate goal was to reunite all five kingdoms, turning them into one unstoppable force.

By doing that, she could restore her world to the utopia that it had once been, back in her younger days, when her father was still alive.

Aden was the key to her success.

Vanessa had not been trying to kill Aden. She knew that this immortal would not die easily. What she had been trying to do was kidnap him.

She thought that she could use his father as blackmail, to convince him to help her, but a wrench had been thrown into her plans when he passed much too quickly, freezing to death in the frigid waters.

Her other reason for trying to capture Aden was simple. As soon as she'd seen Kailani and him together, she knew that she must find a way to separate him from her. The longer they were together, the stronger their bond would become. If Vanessa failed to do this, all would be lost and her plans would be ruined. He was of no use to her dead, no longer able to unite the precious stones.

Vanessa knew in the prophecy Maggie had shared with her, that it was her niece, Kailani, that it had named. The prophecy said it would be her, who ultimately could and would be the one to kill Aden.

CPSIA information can be obtained at www.ICGtesting.com
Printed in the USA
LVOW11*0347070316

478043LV00005B/11/P

9 781478 701378